wipe✗out

To Katy, my mother

Books never just happen to a writer. We always get lots of help (and our families – in my case my wonderful husband, Andy Wadsworth and my baby daughter, Olivia – are always very patient and kind people). This particular book was inspired by an exercise I set my Writing for Young People module at Bath Spa University College. So first of all I need to thank Philip Gross, who was in charge of the module, for letting me teach it and (as always) for his inspiring and uplifting example (on how to write, how to teach and how to live). I would also like to thank Rosie, Chris, Ellin, Trish, Naomi, Vanessa and all my other students. I'm sure I didn't teach them half as much as they did me. Thanks also to all the surfers who helped – the boys of Bournemouth, the Newquay posse – the veterans and the grommies. I hope a real-life Hawaiian Tropic Open Trophy goes into a UK cabinet soon. I owe a huge debt of gratitude to Sophie Gorell-Barnes at MBA – another great agent from a great agency. She has superb instincts as well as a fabulous collection of shoes. Many, many, many thanks to Alison Stanley, my editor, and the whole team at Collins, who made Billy's story look and sound so utterly beautiful and changed things without ever hurting my feelings (not an easy thing to do). And, most importantly, thanks to you, reader, for having faith in them and in me. We'll never try to let you down. Take her easy, dudes.

w1pe⁄out

mimi thebo

An imprint of HarperCollins*Publishers*

First published in Great Britain in hardback by Collins in January 2003
First published in Great Britain in paperback by Collins in July 2003
Collins is an imprint of HarperCollins*Publishers* Ltd
77-85 Fulham Palace Road, Hammersmith, London W6 8JB

The HarperCollins website address is www.**fire**and**water**.com

1 3 5 7 9 8 6 4 2

Text copyright (c) Mimi Thebo 2003

ISBN 000 714277 3

Mimi Thebo asserts the moral right to be
identified as the author of the work.

Printed and bound in Great Britain by
Clays Ltd, St Ives plc

prologue

You know when you're having a nap on a really sunny day and you get this great feeling even before you open your eyes, because the yellow of the sun is coming through your lids? Well, that is happening to me. I can feel how warm it is just by how yellow the light is shining. It's the afternoon, so we must be in Cornwall or Devon, somewhere we had to drive most of the night to get to. Did we just stay up for the morning's surfing? Maybe that's why I'm still tired. I try and think if I've already been in the sea, but all I can concentrate on is the gold coming through my closed eyes.

I'm having a hard time waking up. My eyes flicker open in little bursts. I see the curtains of our VW combi van, bright red checks, sucked in and out of the window in the breeze, and then I close them again. Next time I see the stencils Mum did around the panelling. Then I close them again. I can hear Mum humming to herself, like she does when she's alone, and I can't hear Daddy Cool talking. So I figure we must be in North Devon, because if it was anywhere near Newquay, Daddy Cool would be with us. He always moved heaven and earth to surf with Mum.

In the next little burst I see Mum herself, her eyes all bright and shining, leaning over me. Her skin is brown and she has her hair tied back so that I can see her silver dolphin earrings dangling against her neck.

She's shaking my shoulder and so I make a big effort and wake up properly. The tide must be coming in – it's time to get in the water. I'm already thinking about whether I'll have to wear a wetsuit or not. I'm already thinking about my

6

new board and that move Sloppy showed me last time we surfed North Devon.

But when I open my eyes properly, it's not Mum, it's Dad. And it's not the van. It's not even sunlight: it's that nasty white chemical light you get in these places. Everything in this hallway is white, except for the grey plastic chair I've been sleeping on. My dad says, 'I've finished with the paperwork; we can go now.'

His voice is as flat and colourless as this world I've woken up into. I just want to go back to sleep. But Dad looks even more tired than I am, too tired to try and carry me. And I'm eleven, anyway, too big and too old to be carried. So I get to my feet, somehow, and stumble down the long white hall. I feel like I've been pounded flat. I feel totally wiped out.

1
night driving

The night that Mum went away was as black as the ink on this page. I looked out of the window as Dad sped along the lanes and I couldn't see the moon. I couldn't even see a star.

'Why do I have to go and stay with Auntie Mary?'

Dad swallowed before he spoke and, when he finally did answer, his voice was funny. He said, 'I have a lot to do. It's like last half term, when I was so busy and you went to stay with Auntie Helen.'

'I'd rather stay with Auntie Helen than Auntie Mary,' I said. Anyone would.

Dad did that swallowing thing again. He said, 'I'm sorry, bucko. But I need Auntie Helen to help me. Auntie Mary is going to help you.' And then he said very softly, 'I hope.' I knew I wasn't supposed to hear that, so I pretended that I hadn't.

But I still said, 'I always have to go to Auntie Mary's. I hate it. There's nothing there.'

And Dad said, 'I took a bag of yours over ages ago. It's got clothes and books and things in. A football, I think.'

'You think? How can you not tell if a bag's got a football in it?'

He said, 'I didn't pack it. Your mum did. She wanted you to have... she thought that you might...' And then the most horrible thing happened.

My dad's chin started to wobble. He made a sound like a cough and then his mouth went all crooked and tears started coming out of his eyes. He stopped the Cavalier, just where he was, in the middle of a country lane. Dad was crying. Really crying. Really hard.

Ordinarily, this would have freaked me out completely and I would have done something, hugged him or patted him or something. Anything. But I felt cold inside, as cold as the black, night sky. And I said, 'Then she knew, didn't she?'

'Knew what?'

'Mum knew she was... going away.'

My dad looked at me with tears still running down the stubble on his cheeks. He said, 'She knew, yeah. But she didn't want to, Billy. She didn't want to go away. She didn't want to leave us.'

'She had a bag already packed for me!' I felt like I had swallowed the black night. I didn't think I would ever feel warm inside again.

Dad reached out and held my arm, but I looked out of the window. He said, 'She was always thinking about you, even at the last, even as she was going away—'

But I said, 'Why do we keep saying Mum *went away*? She didn't go away. She died. Mum died, Dad. Mum is dead.'

Dad leaned his head against my arm. He cried and cried. But I just stared out at the black night, my heart as empty and cold as the sky.

I must have fallen asleep. The next thing I remember was waking up, just a little bit, the way you do when you think you might have to go to the bathroom or someone comes in to kiss you goodnight or you're sleeping with someone and they kick you. I *almost* woke up. There was a bright light in my face. I tried to open my eyes, but they were heavy. I just saw a sliver of Dad talking to Auntie Mary. I heard him, too.

He said, 'She just faded away.'

I knew he was talking about Mum and suddenly I could feel again. It hurt so bad I thought I would die from it. Then someone clicked off the light and I sort of passed out, as you would from a broken leg or something, but this was from something else that was broken, something deep in me, something I knew no doctor could mend.

Then it was morning and I was opening my eyes all the way. The sun was a weak grey shadow on the curtains. I got up and pushed them back.

The only good thing about Auntie Mary's house is the view. She has the biggest house in the little town she lives in and it's right up on top of the only hill. You can see the whole valley from the bedroom she always sticks me in.

But that day, you could hardly see a thing.

The blue hills on the horizon were nearly as white as the sky. The green hills close to were a dull grey. The houses were lumps of coal. The lane was the colour of pencil lead and the hedges were the same greeny-grey as bread mould.

Auntie Mary opened the door. She said, 'Oh, good, you're up. It's a terrible misty morning, isn't it?'

She's a grey person herself, Auntie Mary. Her hair is grey. Her teeth are grey. That might be why she always seems to dress in grey. She wore a dark grey tweed skirt and a dark grey cardigan. Her blouse was a dull white. Even her silver brooch looked dull and tarnished.

She had a bath ready for me. She only ever poured about six inches of water and she never put in any bubbles. Her towels were thin and hard and her toothpaste was a dull pink paste that burns your tongue.

When I came back to my room, she had clothes laid out for me. They didn't look like my clothes, though I recognised my underpants and shoes.

The other things were horrible. But she called, 'Breakfast is ready!' from downstairs and I couldn't very well go down in just my pants and shoes. So I put on the black, scratchy trousers and the stiff white shirt and pulled the black jumper over my head. It was furry and smelled funny. The socks were weird, too, woolly. They came all the way up to my knees. There was a black tie lying there as well, on elastic. I left that.

'What are these clothes?' I asked her, as I joined her at the breakfast table.

'They're your mourning,' she said. 'I saw you didn't have any, so I bought you some. I hope the sizes are right. Do they fit?'

I didn't know what to say.

I usually don't know what to say. I'm 'too quiet', according to my school reports.

But my mum used to tell me that's what good manners were for – that as long as you know the *right* thing to say, nobody will mind if you don't say anything else.

So instead of saying, 'Yeah, they fit, but they're really horrible and I hate them,' I said, 'Yes, thank you.' She poured me some orange squash from a jug. It's the kind you make up yourself and she only ever puts a little trickle of syrup in, not even enough to make the water orange.

'Would you like some toast?' she asked. 'I have Marmite or jam.'

'What colour?' I asked.

'Colour?' she said.

'What colour jam?' I asked. And then thought to explain, 'I mean what flavour.'

'Blackcurrant,' she said.

'No, thank you,' I said.

She poured some cornflakes into my bowl

from a big, white box with dull blue printing on it saying 'Budget'. I poured the milk from the jug. It was skimmed, and hardly tasted of milk at all. I don't know how I ate the whole bowl. I must have been hungrier than I thought. I would have had to be.

'What would you like to do today?' Auntie Mary asked. 'We could go for a walk.'

I thought about the grey hills. I said, 'Well...'

She said, 'We could do the shopping.'

I had gone shopping with Auntie Mary before. She always had coupons and looked at the prices of things very, very carefully. The last time I went to the supermarket with Auntie Mary I was just about embarrassed to death at the deli counter when she raised a fuss because the lady had cut three pence more bacon than Auntie Mary had wanted to pay. I said, 'Actually, I'm a bit tired.'

Auntie Mary said, 'Of course. You must be.' She thought for a moment and then seemed to get an idea. 'Your books are in your room,' she said. 'You could lie down on the duvet.

Just for a treat, I'll leave the central heating on all day, eh?'

I said, 'That would be nice, Auntie Mary,' though it didn't seem such a big deal to me. We always had the central heating on all day at our house. I suppose I should tell you now that Auntie Mary isn't poor. She isn't poor at all; she's richer than the rest of us put together. Dad says she's just got into funny ways since Uncle William died. Dad says she used to be lively and a real joy to be with. But that was before I was born. And I don't know if I believe it, anyway.

I went back up the stairs to the room she always sticks me in. It's all done in a powdery blue colour. Not blue like the sky on a sunny day or blue like a robin's egg or blue like the sea or blue like a bluebell. No, this is a kind of dusty blue, a blue that has forgotten what blue ought to be and has decided to try and be grey instead. The walls are that colour. The carpet is that colour. The velvet headboard is that colour. And the curtains and the duvet cover are that colour with a bit of white in a horrible flowery stripe.

It's a depressing room even when nothing is wrong. When your mum has just died, it's the worst place on earth.

2
tsunami

I shut the door. Shut myself into the most depressing room on the planet. Again, I felt cold inside. I went to stand at the window, where I could rest my hands on the radiator and feel it start to come alive. The pipes all through the big old house bubbled and gurgled. I wondered if I would ever come alive again.

Would there be a gurgling sound in me if I did? Ordinarily, thinking something like that would make me smile. It didn't.

Outside, the mist was thicker. Now I couldn't even see the hills that were usually blue, and the hills that were usually green were fading fast. I went to look at myself in the mirror.

Usually, my face stays pretty sunburned about half the year from swimming in the sea and the other half gets kind of rosy from running around a footie pitch in the wind and the rain. So one way or another, I look OK. But I hadn't played much football this term. I'd been going to the hospital too much to train and I hadn't played in an actual match for weeks. My face was pale.

My eyes seemed huge in my face, and had dark smudges all around them, as if I had been wearing make-up or something. I rubbed at them, but they wouldn't come off.

My hair was dull brown.

Mum used to squeeze a lemon on my hair before we went to the beach. She knew about things like that — she was a surfer. She squeezed lemons on her own hair and on mine, too. Then the sun and the sea would make parts of it reddish and parts of it yellowish. By the end of the summer, the ends of my hair would be nearly white. It looked just like hers. It looked amazing.

There was nothing amazing about it now.

There was nothing amazing about me now, wearing these horrible clothes in this horrible room.

It was so quiet I could hear myself breathe.

I wanted to hear music, not just any music, but my mum's kind of music. She used to listen to guitar music, oldey-timey rock and roll stuff, the Ventures, the Beach Boys, Jan and Dean. Sometimes she'd buy newer stuff, but it always sounded like the older stuff. My Dad hated it – called it 'cheesy'. But when she was hoovering or something she'd have it up really loud, dancing around like a mad woman. It was really embarrassing.

Still, I hadn't heard any for months. And now, it was like it was playing in my head, but faintly, like I *just* couldn't hear it. And suddenly I wanted to hear it, wanted to hear those big, twangy guitar chords. Maybe they could wake me up.

But all I heard were the pipes gurgling again.

Auntie Mary had put my books on a horrible little shelf on the wall where she used to keep a horrible row of horrible china sheep. I hated that. It looked as though she had moved me in, as if I was going to stay there forever. I pulled them all off the shelf and stacked them on my bedside table. I opened one up and started to read it. It was very good, but even so, I was asleep before I finished the first chapter.

Have you ever noticed that if you sleep during the day, you dream like crazy? It seemed like I was hardly asleep before I started to dream.

It's summer. And I am waking up in the combi van. I always love having a nap and waking up there. Our combi is panelled inside – yellow with green trim. It has red flowers that Mum had stencilled all the way around. She'd made red cushions to match. I love waking up there so much that I always try and go to sleep again, just so I can do it twice. But I never can. Even in my dream I can't.

'Hey, bucko, tide waits for no man. You coming out with me?' It's Mum, only before she was sick. Her hair is a tangle of colour – brown, blonde, ginger. She is wearing her shortie wetsuit, the one with the big patches of hot pink and orange. She smiles at me and I jump out of my bunk to hug her.

'Hey!' she says, 'No time for smoochie-woochie nonsense, bucko me lad; there's a wave to catch!'

She helps me into my wetsuit and I get my board down.

Under the awning, she stops and bends down to look into my eyes. I can see hers, see the green flecks in the soft brown circles. 'What's the word?' she asks.

'Careful, careful,' I remember to say, even though it's been nearly a year since I've had to say it.

'Take it what?'

'Take it in turns,' I say. 'I watch for you and you watch for me.'

'Never what?'

'Never do anything stupid. If you ever need help, I get some help, I don't jump in.'

She punches me on the point of my chin, just softly, but still enough so that my teeth click together. She says, 'Allrighty!'

We walk to where the waves are beating and they are big, really big, really way too big for me. She would have never let me suit up in surf like that. Still, in my dream, she lets me. In my dream, she will let me go out in that sea, with waves higher than three men, higher than two VW combi vans.

I can feel the shingle under my boots, feel it hard and shifting. I can hear my breathing. I can feel the wind moving my hair around. I lick my lips and taste the salt.

We stop near the edge of the water and put down our boards. We do scissors, paper, stone to see who gets to go first and the sea is so far up that when I lose I am relieved. I never thought I would ever be afraid of a big wave, but in my dream it's like I'm really there. I can see just how big they are and how rough the breakers are. It's not like sitting safe in your lounge and looking at a magazine and thinking, 'I'd like to have a go on that.' It's real. And it's pretty intimidating.

But not to Mum. She runs out and slices through the breakers, swimming so hard and so sure that she looks more like a dolphin or a seal than somebody's mother.

I lose her for a moment, but then I can see her and she's sitting on her board, rising and falling with the swells. She's kicking her feet like she does when she's really excited, and her leash is whipping around. A couple of big waves really lift her, but she lets them go. And then she must see something I don't, because she drops down in a hurry and paddles further out as if she's got to hustle to make something.

And then I see it.

It's a monster. A big, grey wave, white at the top. It curls over into a whacking big tube, like those waves they have in Hawaii or Australia. And Mum is paddling like anything, I just know she's going to take it on. I start to shout, 'Be careful!' but of course she can't hear me.

And then suddenly she's riding it and she's in perfect position, just on top, just moving along the crest. She's all angled to drop down and nip under the curl. But she doesn't. For some reason, she doesn't. It's like she's stuck on top of the crest, like she's been superglued or something. She doesn't even look like she's moving.

It's not normal.

And the wave isn't normal either. Instead of getting smaller, it's getting bigger, like a tidal wave, like something out of a movie. As it moves towards the shore, it's getting bigger and bigger and now it's bigger than our house. Now it's bigger than Auntie Mary's house – it's as tall as a church. Now it's as tall as a skyscraper. I look up and I can still see Mum. She hasn't moved at all; she's still up there, stuck on the crest.

And then the big grey wave is towering over me and I am looking up at a wall of dense, dark water. It's a tidal wave, a tsunami.

And then it crashes, so cold. And I stop breathing. I still have my eyes open, and I can see Mum in the wave, but she's so cold that her face is grey. Then I look down and I'm all grey. I'm still in the wave, but I can walk to the combi van. It's all grey, too. No green paint, no red stripy awning, no yellow towels waiting on the railing. It's all grey. Grey paint, grey stripes, even grey towels. I turn back to try and see Mum, but she's fading, fading. She reaches out to me, and I try and take her hand, but it fades even as I touch it and I'm only holding water.

I don't know what I was screaming.

'William? William!' When I opened my eyes, Auntie Mary was sitting on the bed. 'It's a dream,' she said. Her hand moved towards me and awkwardly pushed my hair back out of my eyes before retreating on to her lap. 'It's only a dream.'

'But Mum was...'

She smiled at me and took off her glasses to polish them on a hanky she kept up the sleeve of her cardigan. It was the first time I'd ever seen her eyes without them. I remember being really surprised by how blue they were, so much bluer than that horrible room. She said, 'It's only to be expected, William. You'll have been thinking about her, you see.'

And then we sat there for a few moments. She put her glasses back on and then twisted her handkerchief around. I could see how nervous she was.

I said, 'What time is it?'

'Nearly two. I popped my head around the door at lunchtime, but I didn't want to wake you.' She twisted for a few more moments. 'Are you hungry?'

And you know, I was, despite the nightmare, despite everything. 'Very,' I said.

'Shall we have another little treat? Shall we go to the fish bar? They fry until half past.'

I don't like to eat fish. I mean I really don't like to eat fish. Not like not liking Brussels sprouts, where you can force them down if you have to, but much, much worse. Completely unforcedownable. I opened my mouth to say something about this to Auntie Mary, but she had whipped out a bit of paper from her cardigan pocket. She read from what seemed to be a list and then said, 'Of course, they do burgers as well.'

'Like McDonald's?' I asked.

'I believe so,' Auntie Mary said. 'But then I've never been to a McDonald's.'

We walked pretty quickly down Auntie Mary's lane and through the little town to the high street. Every time I go walking with Auntie Mary I get reminded that she's not as old as she looks. Sometimes, I really have to work to keep up with her.

The mist was so thick that other people looked like ghosts. When we opened the door to the fish shop, there was the silver tinkle of a little bell.

'Why, Mrs Montague!' The fish lady had bleached hair and a big white overall. The whole shop was white – white counter, white lino with lots of footprints, white tables, white chairs. 'I'd never expect to see you on a Wednesday! Friday's usually you. And for lunch, as well!'

Auntie Mary seemed flustered. 'Well, there's a lot going on up at the house,' she said, rather grandly, as if 'the house' was terribly important.

'Ah,' the fish lady said and goggled at me. 'So, it's come to that, has it?'

I knew she was talking about Mum and I had another one of those moments when I could actually feel something. I felt like I wanted to kill the fish lady. I didn't want anyone else to even *think* about my mum.

Auntie Mary answered sharply, 'One small cod with chips and one burger with chips, please.'

'Will the little man have salt and vinegar?' the fish lady asked Auntie Mary, as if I was too young to speak for myself. If anything, that made me want to kill her more. I mean, I know I'm a bit small for my age, but I am eleven years old. I've been ordering for myself since I was about four.

I asked, 'Do you have any ketchup?' but was

surprised by how soft my voice came out, all hoarse and kind of squeaky.

'What was that?'

Auntie Mary swelled up like an angry balloon. 'He asked you if you had tomato sauce,' she boomed in her grandest accent, much too loud for the little shop.

But the fish lady didn't notice how grand Auntie Mary was being. She scratched her head and thought for a moment. Then she kind of hunched over and spoke to me in a strange, singing kind of voice. 'No,' she said. 'No tomato sauce, I'm afraid.'

'Then salt and vinegar, please,' I said, and was glad that my voice came out all right this time.

'Salad?' the fish lady asked. 'Mayonnaise?'

Auntie Mary sighed with impatience.

'Yes,' I said. 'Everything.'

'Will that be for here or to take away?'

'Take away,' Auntie Mary and I said together, though we had planned to eat it there.

Instead, we ate at the kitchen table. My

burger was grey and the 'salad' was only pale lettuce and some onion. The mayonnaise was greasy and horrible. But the chips were all right.

Auntie Mary munched in silence. Finally, she said, 'I was not impressed with that, not impressed at all. That batter tasted stale.'

I said, 'The chips aren't bad.'

But she said, 'For those prices not bad isn't good enough.' And then she sniffed. 'And the impertinence! Our family is our business.'

'Too right,' I said.

'Too right is right,' Auntie Mary agreed. She sniffed again and shook her head sharply. 'There's a McDonald's near the supermarket. Let's give them our custom tomorrow, what do you say? We could get the car out and go whenever we liked.'

'They do a fish sandwich,' I said.

'Do they now?' Auntie Mary said. 'Think of that.'

'Could we go tonight?' I was just thinking about McDonald's, about how much of it is bright red and bright yellow plastic. It was like I was craving colour, like I needed colour much more than I needed food or water.

'I've been meaning to speak to you about this evening,' Auntie Mary said. 'I belong to a club which has regular meetings and one of them is tonight.'

'Oh,' I said.

'Now, I could think of two things to do. Either I could stay home with you and we could play some games, perhaps Cluedo or Monopoly...'

Whatever the other option was, I hoped it was better than that. I crossed my fingers for luck under the table.

'Or,' Auntie Mary said, 'you could come along to the meeting. We're having a speaker tonight, a naturalist, someone who goes to terribly exotic places and takes pictures of animals. I believe there is a slide show. I've checked with the secretary and it would be fine for you to accompany me, if you like.'

Slide show, I thought, animals, exotic locations. There should be lots of colours there

– green jungles with brightly-feathered parrots, stripy tigers.

'I'd rather see the slide show' I said, and then remembered another polite thing to say. 'It was nice of you to ask if I could come along.'

'Are you sure?' Auntie Mary asked me. 'You aren't just trying to make *me* feel happy, are you?'

'No,' I said. I was trying to make me feel happy. Make me feel anything at all.

3
walk, don't run

Getting the car out was always a bit of a hassle at Auntie Mary's and I was glad we didn't have to. I was glad, though, to be with Auntie Mary as we walked along the gloomy, fog-bound lanes and streets. Not because I was at all frightened of the shifting shapes that loomed and twisted in the dank mist, no, not at all. But it was nice to have someone nearby you, someone who knew where they were going.

The slide show was at the vicar's house, but when we got to the bottom of the hill, we didn't turn towards the church. I said, 'Are you sure you can see where you're going, Auntie Mary?'

But she answered, 'Oh, goodness, William, don't you worry. I could find my way around this town blindfolded.' So I didn't say anything else.

We ended up at a house on the edge of town, where the fields started. I hadn't walked this way for a long time and I was sure I had never seen this particular house. I would have remembered if I had. It was the kind of house you would remember.

It was long and low and the trees hung over it as if they had been planted just to shelter it. Large, biscuit-coloured squares leaked light into the misty night from walls that looked like big boxes some giant had thrown down in a heap. It was black – black steel, black stone and a black slate roof. Even the pebbles in the path up the garden were dark. And the door where Auntie Mary rang the bell was a huge square slab of black wood.

When we came in, the light was dim and there was a big fuss about taking off coats and remembering to stuff the scarves up the sleeves. When I could finally look around I saw a huge expanse of room with black windows on the other side. No curtains, no carpet, not even any plaster on the walls. Everything was bare, bare stone, bare slate. I said to Auntie Mary, 'This isn't the vicarage.'

And above me tinkled a little silver laugh. 'Oh my, no!' It was a thin woman dressed all in black. Her hair was black, too, except for one streak of white at the front. Around her neck was the white collar a priest wears.

'This is our new vicar, William,' Auntie Mary said. 'Mrs Polinger.'

'You can call me Rachel,' the thin vicar said. 'Everyone does.'

I put out my hand and had it shaken. I said, 'Nice to meet you,' but my eyes roamed around the big, strange room.

'I think you're nearly the last,' the vicar said. 'Shall we have a quick natter in the kitchen about club business, Mary? Stephen will be glad to show William around the house, if he's interested.'

I heard Auntie Mary say, 'He certainly *looks* interested,' and shut my mouth where I had left it hanging open.

'Would you like that, William?' a short, tubby man with grey hair said to me. 'I'm Stephen. I'm Rachel's husband. I made this house.'

I didn't say anything, but I followed him as he walked to the big black windows across the slate floor. He spoke a lot about the view and how he had tried to make the house look like it had sprung out of the ground naturally, but there was nothing natural about the house to me. I saw the bedrooms, the bathrooms and how the showers worked. I saw the dining room and the study and came back to the big, big lounge. There wasn't a spot of colour anywhere. Everything was stone or rope or glass or natural cotton.

The only good thing was a big fire in a huge, square basket in the middle of the big, big lounge. The chimney wasn't attached to a wall, like a normal chimney. It floated above the fire instead. There was a big, slate, bench-like thing that ran around the edge of the fire basket. It was warm and the fire danced yellow and red. I leaned on the warm slates and watched the fire dance.

'Do you like the fireplace?' the vicar's husband asked.

I nodded. I was too busy watching the flames to try and think of something to say.

Someone joined us, another man, but this one wasn't short and wasn't tubby. He was tall and tanned and had blond hair. 'Mark,' the vicar's husband said to him, 'I finally found someone who likes my fireplace. Rogers said it ruined the place, made it look like a ski chalet.'

They laughed. Then Stephen explained to me, 'I build houses for a living and I've just started designing them as well. The architects I used to pay don't think much of my skills in design.'

I asked, 'Are all the houses you do like this? Doesn't anybody want carpets or curtains?'

And this made them laugh again.

Just then, Auntie Mary came back from the kitchen in a swarm of women and again there was a bit of a fuss, this time about making sure the lighting was right for the slide show. We all went down into a little pit on one side of the big, big lounge, where there were lots of very long, very black sofas. I was between Auntie Mary and the end of the sofa, right in front of a square screen that let down from the ceiling. 'That's their telly,' Auntie Mary said. 'They have a projection television.' I could tell she was dead impressed.

I wasn't.

I didn't like the room, I didn't like Stephen and I didn't much care for the vicar. But when the big blond man began to speak, he was Australian and that made me like him because my mum loved Australia and my mum and my dad met there. She used to say that she and my dad made me there, that I was made in Australia. I'm going to go there someday myself. I got all caught up in thinking about this and missed Mark's introduction. The next thing I knew he was clicking something in his hand that made a square of light appear on the big screen.

I was excited. I was going to see animals, the jungle. And I was so close to the screen it was going to be like being bathed in colour. Mark clicked again.

A picture came up. It was of a snowfield, a huge expanse of snow. In the middle of it all was a little tiny green hut, nearly covered in the cold white snow. 'This was where we lived and did all our developing,' Mark said. 'It got pretty cosy sometimes, I can tell you.'

All the ladies laughed.

But I didn't laugh. It was like a bad joke. Slide after slide. White snow, dark grey sea, black seals, black and white penguins. No colour at all, not a single leaf of green. I stopped listening and then I stopped looking.

'William.' Auntie Mary's voice was slow and kind. I stirred and blinked and opened my eyes. We were all alone in the pit of the big, big lounge. I had fallen asleep again. Everyone else was up by the fireplace.

'Do you want to stay for something to eat?'

Auntie Mary asked. 'Or shall we be getting home?'

'Home,' was all I could bring myself to say. I didn't even remember to say 'please'. I didn't like it there. I wished I hadn't come.

'All right then,' Auntie Mary said. 'Thank Stephen and Rachel while I get our coats.'

I felt my hair, but luckily I hadn't slept on it and it wasn't sticking up anywhere. I rubbed my eyes and looked until I could find the vicar and her husband.

'William!' the vicar said kindly. 'Are you off?' And I decided that I liked her after all. She held out her hand and I shook it again. She said, 'It was lovely to meet you at last. Your Aunt Mary has told me so much about you.'

'Has she?' I was surprised.

'Oh my, yes!' The vicar's sharp, black eyes twinkled in her face. 'All about how you can surf and how well you play football and how when you took up the recorder you could play two tunes the very first day.'

I went red. I didn't know Auntie Mary even

knew all that about me, let alone that she spoke of it to anyone else. The vicar tousled my hair. Usually, I hate that, but just then it felt all right. I said, 'Thank you,' and I suppose I meant it for everything.

Then I went over to find Stephen. He was talking to Mark and it took a moment for him to notice me. That gave me time to think of what to say, so when he turned to me I was ready. 'Thank you for letting me see your house,' I said.

Stephen put out his hand and I shook it. 'No problem,' he said.

Now all through this, all the other ladies were talking and chatting. There were ten or twelve of them, all kinds of ladies: old ones like Auntie Mary and quite young ones in trendy clothes. But just then they all must have felt thirsty or hungry or run out of things to say, because just then, just when it shouldn't have, it got very, very quiet.

'No need to thank *me*,' Mark said. 'Sorry I was so boring. I know I can go on about my work, but I've never actually put anyone to sleep before.'

If I thought my face had gone red when the vicar spoke to me, I was wrong. This was what it really felt like when your face goes red. I have never been so embarrassed in my entire life. Everyone heard. Everyone. I looked at the awful, bare, slate floor and my eyes filled with tears. I didn't cry, they didn't quite spill over, but they felt like they wanted to. I thought if I just kept looking down, I could hold them all in.

In a much colder voice than he had used with me, I heard Stephen say, 'Mark, can I have a word?' And the two of them moved away. All the ladies started to talk extra loud, as if they hadn't heard.

Somehow, without looking up, I managed to find my way towards the door, where Auntie Mary had my coat waiting. I pushed my arms in.

'Hold on, mate.'

It was Mark. He bent down to look in my face. He said, 'I'm awful sorry, mate, I didn't know. I shouldn't have ribbed you like that.'

And then my eyes spilled over. Mark grabbed my arm and pulled me into the cloakroom. He sat me down on the lid of the silver toilet. I cried quite a while, not like Dad had, not moaning or groaning. Just tears falling down my face. Mark squatted on his heels on the slate floor and leaned against the stone wall. He didn't do anything. He just waited.

When I stopped, he rummaged around in a cupboard and found a black flannel. He handed it to me and I washed my face.

'Ready to go out?' he asked.

I shook my head, no. I sat back down on the toilet lid and he settled back down on his heels.

'Animals do that,' he said.

'Do what?'

'Sleep when they're hurt. Especially young ones. I've seen seals where a whale has taken a good chunk out of them. They just curl up on the ice pack. You think they're dead, but they aren't. They're healing. A couple of days later, they get up and flop back into the sea.'

'Good as new?' I asked.

Mark sighed. 'No,' he said. 'Not as good as new. They're still missing the chunk. But they can still swim and hunt and stuff.'

I said, 'I'm ready to go now.'

And he said, 'Let's go, then.'

I went back out into the hall and Auntie Mary looked worried. I got back into my coat and wound my scarf around my throat. Mark walked us as far as the lane and he said something to Auntie Mary, something she liked, because she took his arm and patted it, just like she sometimes does to me.

I thought after all that I wouldn't be able to sleep. But Auntie Mary made us some thin, grey cocoa with her thin, grey milk and by the time I had brushed my teeth and climbed into my pyjamas I was yawning again. I got into bed without even putting on the light, so that I didn't have to see the horrible blue-grey room and then I slept and slept, just like a wounded seal on the ice pack of Antarctica.

4
miserlou

I know I'm dreaming. Somehow, I know I'm dreaming. But even though that's true, it's also true that everything feels really, really real.

Again, I lick my lips and taste the salt. I'm on the beach again and my mum and I are doing scissors, paper, stone again. The sea is huge once more. I look back at the combi, though, and it's still nice and bright. The yellow towels are snapping like flags in the wind. I'm not as worried about the sea this time, because I know I'm going to lose scissors, paper, stone. And I do.

My mum punches my scissors with her stone and then she kisses me on my cheek. I can smell her, smell that orange and patchouli oil stuff that she makes up herself and uses instead of perfume. Whenever she made it, the whole house smelled for days. Dad used to say it was like living with a witch. Just like I know that I'm dreaming, I know I'll never smell that stuff again and I reach out to hug her so that I can smell it some more.

But she's gone.

She's dancing through the foam and bellying down on her board to paddle out.

You can't imagine how small Mum could look on her boards. She liked to use boards that everyone said were really too big for her, some of the longest boards on the women's circuit. When you see her in photos on one of them, it looks like her picture was cut out and pasted on to another picture. You just can't imagine her using them. But she carved out some mighty lines with her logs, even though she used smaller ones to compete. But all that's not really interesting, I suppose, if you don't like surfing. But to me, it meant something that she was on a log. And I can't explain it any other way.

I see her slicing out through the breaks again. It's kind of rocky here. I'm sure I've been here before with her. But the waves are huge and it's not cold, just windy. It's not natural.

It gets even less natural when my mum stands up on her board. Not like she's jumping to a crouch, not like she's even getting a wave. Her part of the sea sort of rises up and she stands up on her board with her knees locked. It's stupid. In real life she'd be eating salt water in about a nanosecond, but in this dream she can do that.

I can see her face and she's laughing, but it's not a nice laugh. It's like she's laughing *at* me. She stretches out her hands and she starts to glow, really bright. The colours on her wetsuit start to throb like neon. Her hair stands up all around her head like a lion's or something and it gets really, really bright.

And then I look around and I can see that my mum is stealing all the colour from the whole world for herself. She's up on this platform of sea and it's all running to her arms. Even the blue patches on my wetsuit are fading to grey, the combi's going all grey again, the grass is fading, the sky is fading... everything is fading. And my mum is doing it on purpose. And laughing about it, like it was really, really cool.

And I get this taste in my mouth. I want to scream at her, or cry or stop her, or do *something*, but I know I can't. I just stand there on the shore and watch my mum take the colour out of the world and leave me with nothing.

I woke up gasping, like I'd been underwater again. It was dark in my horrible room. And cold. I reached over and clicked on the light and then clicked it off again. It was the kind of room that doesn't make you feel any better in the light.

I lay there and wondered about my dream. I knew it was just a dream, but my mum had been acting like such a cow in it, stealing all that colour just for herself. I mean, I knew Mum wasn't really like that, but still... I was kind of angry about it. But only kind of. I thought about the smell of her home-made perfume, too, the way her lips were chapped again and rough on my cheek where she'd kissed me. I lay there wondering just *what* I felt about it and the next thing I knew Auntie Mary was opening the curtains and I had another day to face.

'We have a busy day today,' Auntie Mary said when I came downstairs. 'I have my bits and bobs to do around the house. I've been that excited about you coming to stay that I haven't hoovered for days. We'll be covered in dust if I don't jump to it this morning.'

'Can I help?'

'Do you do any housework at home?'

I thought about this. Dad had hired a cleaner when Mum got really ill. I never saw the cleaner. She came when I was at school. I said, 'Sometimes I load the dishwasher.'

Auntie Mary laughed. It was good to hear her

laugh; it was a warm, treacly sound. She said, 'These are my dishwashers,' and held up her hands. I had never really looked at her hands before. She had long fingers, like my dad. I reached out and touched her diamond ring.

'Is that real?' I asked.

'Yes,' she said. 'William always liked to give me jewels. You should see some of my earrings.' She put her hand out on the table so that I could see the little cup of gold that held the diamond up. I don't know anything about jewellery, but you could see whoever made it knew what they were doing.

'I thought we could have boiled eggs with soldiers this morning,' Auntie Mary changed the subject. She fished a piece of paper out of her cardigan pocket and looked at it for a moment and then said, 'You like your eggs on the hard side, don't you?'

'Yes.'

She laid the table, put the knives and forks out and the stiff, white, cloth napkins, and put a juice glass before me.

I looked down at all this and saw the furry black jumper. I hadn't even thought about not putting it on this morning. I thought of them now as my seal clothes. Somehow, those horrible scratchy trousers and that horrible furry jumper and even those horrible long woolly socks felt *right*. I felt like I *should* look horrible, like I *should* be colourless. It was how I felt inside. Why not let everyone know?

But there were limits to the whole colourless thing and one of the limits was orange squash. Auntie Mary had put some water on to boil and then had the jug ready to make squash. When I said, 'Could I make that?' she was surprised.

'Yes, all right.'

I nearly jumped out of my chair. I said, 'If you pour the water in first, *then* put the squash in, you can tell how much to put in.' I went over and filled the jug at the tap and didn't even splash much on my jumper. 'See?' I said. I made the water in the jug go nice and orange. 'You always get it right that way.'

I poured us both a glass and only spilled a

drop and that was on my side of the table. We tasted it and Auntie Mary smiled. 'That is nicer,' she admitted.

'Pure orange juice is even nicer,' I said.

'We have to do some shopping today,' she said. 'We'll get some.'

The water came to the boil and she put the eggs in and set the timer. I drank my squash and watched the timer click around while Auntie Mary made toast under the grill. She buttered the toast with margarine. The margarine tub looked just like the cornflakes box. It was that same dullish white with greyish-blue writing on the side, saying 'Budget'.

Our egg timer went 'ding' and Auntie Mary got the eggs into the cups and cut our toast into soldiers. For a while I was busy eating. I couldn't help but notice that the margarine wasn't very nice, though. It tasted kind of piggy, not like butter at all.

Auntie Mary was reading a newspaper while she ate, and drinking a cup of tea. I watched her, thinking about the big diamond and all the earrings and how she bought the cheapest, nastiest milk and orange and cornflakes and margarine and didn't run her central heating all day until I just couldn't take it any more.

So I said, 'Auntie Mary?'

And she folded her newspaper and put it down. 'Yes?' she said when this was done.

I thought I'd start off with some manners. I said, 'It's nice of you to have me here. When Dad is so busy and everything.'

'You're welcome any time, William.'

'Thank you.' It wasn't an easy thing to say. I tried again. 'You aren't poor, are you, Auntie Mary? Dad says you've got pots of dough.'

Her lips pushed together as though she was trying not to smile. 'I think my brother exaggerates just a little bit,' she said. 'But, no, William, I'm not poor. Your Uncle William left me quite comfortably off. He was the type of man who thinks about things like that.'

I said, 'He must have been nice.'

She said, 'He was lovely.'

And we were stuck again.

Then Auntie Mary said, 'Would you like to see some photographs?' I nodded and she left the kitchen for a moment and came back with an album. She pushed aside our breakfast things any old how and pulled a chair close to mine.

When she opened the album it was like a world of colour leapt off the page. Every day seemed to be summer. She pointed out Uncle William. He was tall and blond and looked a little like Mark. He was standing next to a glamorous woman with glossy brown hair. 'Who's *that*?' I asked.

'That's me.'

I tried not to look as surprised as I felt, but something in my face made Auntie Mary laugh. It wasn't her warm, treacly laugh though. This one was as bitter as lemons.

'There's my dad!' At least he looked the same. Not *just* the same, of course, his hair in the photo was different and he had some funny clothes on. But still, you could tell it was my dad. I wondered why I could recognise my dad but not Auntie Mary. Then I thought, and said, 'You aren't wearing glasses in any of these photos.'

'I used to wear contact lenses.'

'Do you still have them?'

'I might have a pair somewhere.'

I didn't think it was smart to say any more. I flipped through pages and pages. Sometimes my dad was with them and sometimes he wasn't. Sometimes they were in England and sometimes they were somewhere else, Paris, Egypt, even Japan. I remembered our holiday to Majorca last year, just before Mum had got sick.

Auntie Mary had come with us. I remembered Mum saying to Dad that we should have her because 'she never goes anywhere'. Well, she used to go anywhere. She used to go everywhere.

I turned another page and it was a garden party. My dad was with a tall, blonde woman. 'Who's *that*?'

'Your dad's old girlfriend. Cathy.' I peered at the photo.

'How long did he go out with her?' I asked.

'Ages,' Auntie Mary said. 'When she married Philip, it broke your dad's heart. That's why he went out to Australia in the first place. To get over Cathy.'

I flipped through another set of pages, this time of New York. Then there was another garden party and another woman with my dad. My mum.

'She was so beautiful,' Auntie Mary said. 'Not classically beautiful, like Cathy. But she just radiated life. I fell in love with her almost as quickly as your dad did.'

I flipped another page, but it was all black. I turned over more and more pages, but they were all black and bare. Except for three photos, not even stuck in. They were all of me.

'William died in a car accident that same year. And when your mum had you, your dad gave you his name.'

Auntie Mary laid the three photos out carefully.

'Here you are when you were just born,' she said. All I could see was a scrunched-up, raw-looking face coming out of a blanket. 'You were a beautiful baby,' she said.

I thought to myself, No, I wasn't!

The next one was me in Auntie Mary's garden, riding a trike. My hair was still blond and Mum was running behind me. 'That's my favourite,' Auntie Mary said.

'I like it, too.'

The last one was when we were on holiday in Majorca. And I could remember it, remember my mum asking the waiter to take a picture of us all together. Mum and Dad were holding up wine glasses on either end and Auntie Mary and I were in the middle. Auntie Mary was tanned and smiling. She had taken her glasses off and was wearing a pink blouse. And you could see she was the same woman who had looked so glamorous before. We both stared at the photographs for a long time.

And then I just said it. I said, 'Why do you buy such horrible food?'

'What?' Auntie Mary twitched the list out of her pocket and ran over it again. 'I thought you liked egg and soldiers.'

'It's not that.'

I went to the counter and held up the tub of margarine. 'It's all this budget stuff. Why do you buy it?'

'It's a little hard to explain,' Auntie Mary said. She folded the photo album shut and tucked my photos in it again. I waited.

'Well,' she said finally, 'I always try and save money.'

'Why? You have pots of dough.'

'That's not a very nice expression.'

'Sorry.'

'No, I'm sorry.' Auntie Mary pulled her handkerchief out of the sleeve of her cardigan and began twisting it around her fingers. I felt bad now, bad that I had started this, bad that I had made her nervous again.

. 'I shouldn't have said anything,' I said, 'I mean, it's your money.'

'I don't think of it as my money,' Auntie Mary said. 'I think of it as *your* money. I'm going to give it all to you.'

5

underwater

'What?' I said.

'I'm going to give it all to you. The money, the house.' Auntie Mary smiled sadly, 'Even my diamond ring, I suppose, though that will probably go to your wife.'

'Why me?'

'Why not?'

I couldn't stand up any more. My knees felt wobbly. I sat down where Auntie Mary had been sitting before. 'When?' I asked and it made Auntie Mary laugh again, her true, treacly laugh.

'When I die, of course,' she said. This made

my throat close off. I really didn't want anybody else to die, not even Auntie Mary.

She must have seen the fear on my face because she added, 'But that won't be for years and years and years and years and years. Doctor Adkins says I'm as healthy as a horse.'

I thought about all this for a moment. It was a lot to take in. While I thought, Auntie Mary looked at some of the photos again. Finally, I said, 'If you are going to live for years and years and years and years and years, are you going to eat that horrible margarine and drink that horrible milk the whole time?'

I had never seen Auntie Mary really laugh, not like she laughed now. She laughed so much her shoulders shook. She laughed so much I thought she might fall out of her chair. She had to take her glasses off in the end, and wipe her eyes.

At last she stopped and smiled at me, a really big grin. And you know, her teeth aren't all *that* grey, not really. And she said, 'We're going shopping today. And since it's your money, we'll spend it your way. How's that?'

Which made me smile. Which then made me feel a little funny, as if I shouldn't smile, as if I shouldn't have this warm feeling around my heart, not when my mum had just died.

Auntie Mary said, 'But first I need to see to this house of yours. Why don't you go into the lounge and watch some telly? I've already done in there. And I've put the fire on.'

And so I went down the hall and into the lounge. I suppose it was *my* hall and *my* lounge. In a way.

I flicked through the channels, which didn't take long. There were only five of them. Auntie Mary didn't have cable or a satellite dish or even a digital box. I was watching a stupid cartoon and maybe I had the sound up too loud because I didn't hear the doorbell go or anyone knock on the door. I just looked up and saw Mark standing there.

I turned off the telly and stood up.

He said, 'Hey mate, how goes it?'

'I'm fine,' I said.

We stood there for a second and then I remembered to say, 'Would you like to sit down?' and we did. Then I remembered to say, 'Would you like a cup of tea or anything?'

And Mark said, 'Golly, you've got amazing manners.'

I shrugged. I said, 'Mum taught me things to say.'

We both grinned.

'I don't need a cuppa,' Mark said. 'I'm not stopping. I just came by to see how you were getting on.'

'I'm OK.'

'Good. Watching telly?'

I shrugged again. 'Auntie Mary's cleaning up. We're going shopping later.'

'Sounds good.'

'Suppose so.'

'What do you like to do best?'

'Play football. But really, I like to surf.'

'That's what Rachel was telling me; she said you were a surfer. Where do you go?'

'Croyde Bay mainly.'

'What, Devon? That's a fair trek, isn't it? Don't you live in Wiltshire?'

I nodded, 'Yeah, but we used to go all over. We have a combi van. You can sleep in it and everything.'

I thought for a moment. 'At least we did,' I said. 'I didn't end up going much last year.'

Mark shrugged. 'Well, you wouldn't have,' he said.

We sat quiet for a moment, but it wasn't awful. With some people it's awful when you get quiet. It's even a bit awful with Dad sometimes. But it wasn't now. Finally, I thought of something I wanted to say. 'My mum used to go to Australia every year,' I said. 'She was a real surfer, a pro.'

'I didn't know that,' Mark sounded surprised.

'Yeah,' I said, 'that's where my dad met her.'

'Is he a surfer, too?'

'No,' I said. 'He sells carpets.'

We were quiet again for a moment and then Mark said, 'I used to follow a bit of surfing on the telly. What was your mum's name?'

'Meg Archer,' I said, before I remembered. 'No, it would have been Meg Brown. I think they called her Kitten Brown.'

'Your mum was Kitten Brown?' Mark sounded surprised.

'Yeah,' I said.

'She won the Hawaiian Tropic Open one year.'

'Yeah,' I said. 'We've got the trophy.'

'She was brilliant,' Mark said. 'Everybody said she'd never make it, because she was so little, but she was a little tiger. I saw her once on a longboard. I just couldn't believe it. A real little tiger.'

'I s'pose that's why they called her Kitten.'

We got quiet again.

I said, 'I'm kind of from Australia, too. My mum says I was made in Australia.'

Mark said, 'Were you now? Well, that explains a lot.' But he didn't say what it explained. We sat for a while longer and then he stood up. 'I'm meant to give you this.' It was a card with Rachel's address and phone number written on it, a business card. No one had ever given me a business card before.

'Rachel and Stephen say that if you need anything or even if you just want to talk, be sure and give them a buzz.' He walked to the door and then he said, 'I'm staying there for a couple of days, too.'

I stood up again. I said, 'Thank you for coming.'

He shook his head. 'I've never seen the like,' he said. 'You've got the best manners of any kid I've ever met. I'll see you around.'

And then he was gone and I was left with the card in my hand. I put it in my pocket. I thought that's what I was probably supposed to do with it.

I turned the television back on and the cartoon was over. It was a decorating programme. They were showing the before and the after. The before was a horrible lounge, kind of like the one I was sitting in, dark and dull. The after was brilliant, a really nice warm orangey colour. Then a lady came and talked about how they did it. She said that there were orangey bits in the curtains and the furniture before, but that the paint was so horrible it made them go all dull.

Then they showed these two men who came in and rolled the carpet back and took all the furniture out. They took the curtains down and covered the floor with cloth. And then they painted the walls. After that was done, they put down an orangey coloured carpet and put the curtains and the furniture back in. And the room looked amazing.

The lady said that if you have a dull room, look closely at the curtains and cushion covers before you throw them away. She says there might be hidden jewels of colour in a dull pattern that the right paint would bring right out.

I went over and looked carefully at Auntie Mary's horrible lounge curtains. They had a kind of large diamond pattern in a dull greeny-gold. But inside the diamonds were flowers. I looked at the flowers closely. They were a purpley-bluey colour. And then I went to the sofa and looked at it closely. It, too, was a dark greeny-gold, like the carpet, like the horrible, striped wallpaper. But if you looked really closely, there was the same purpley-bluey colour there, too, swirled into the centre of the swirly circles of velvet. I put my eye really, really close to the fabric. And then I fell asleep.

I open my eyes and I'm in the VW van again. And now, I'm not even happy about that, I'm not even happy about seeing the flowers and everything. I'm not even happy about the sunshine that's flooding through the windows and blowing out the red and white checked curtains. Because I know it's a dream and that something awful is about to happen to me in this dream. So I can't even get happy about my favourite thing. Which is a real pain.

But I can't help but get happy to see my mum again. She's all suited up in her shortie and her hair is tied back. She's ready for action. She nuzzles my neck and I try to hold on to her. She says something, but I can't hear what. I can't hear in this one. I can only hear the crash of the waves on the breakwater outside. And then she pushes me away.

I get into my wetsuit and follow her out again. This time I don't even bother to take my board down. I know I won't be going in.

The surf is huge. Mum plunges in and starts swimming out. But this time she stops halfway, just to look back and wave at me. She's grinning.

And even though I know something horrible is going to happen, I can't help but grin and wave back. She just looks so happy. And it's so cool to see her well again and strong again, like she was just six months ago. Before she faded away.

If you saw her in my dream, you couldn't imagine she could *ever* fade away. She's cutting through the breakers, so sure and strong. And then she's through and sitting on her board again, riding the swells and kicking her legs, making her lead dance.

This time a really big wave comes in and lifts her up, but she doesn't get up to ride it. She just sits on her board. That would be weird enough, but what's really weird is that the wave doesn't move. It just lifts her up, higher and higher, until she's sitting up on a mountain of a wave.

And then she stretches her arms out and does that horrid, colour-stealing thing again. The bad taste comes back into my mouth. I look around me and, again, the shingle goes all one grey, the combi goes grey, my suit goes grey, even the grass on the hills behind us. And I look at my mum and she's got all the colour inside her – she's glowing so bright it's like looking into the sun.

But then it all starts to leak out of the rails of her board. Either side, a big slick of colour is coming down from her wave. The whole sea is being coloured by Mum. It's bizarre. And suddenly, I feel like something cool is about to happen, something really, really good. But then the whole dream starts fading and as much as I try to stay there, something pulls me back, back, into Auntie Mary's horrible lounge.

6
over the edge

It was someone shouting.

'He looks horrible, Mary! What the hell have you done to my son?'

It was my dad shouting. I'd heard him shout before, plenty of times, usually down the phone to suppliers, occasionally at Mum, and more than once at me. I always hated it.

I couldn't hear what Auntie Mary said in reply. But I could just hear the sound of her talking.

'Mourning? He's only eleven years old – he's just a bleeding kid! He looks like something out of *Oliver Twist*!'

I opened the lounge door. They weren't in the hall. It sounded like they were in the kitchen.

Again, I could just hear the sound of Auntie Mary answering, but not make out any words. Until I actually got to the kitchen door, which was open a crack. The hallway was dark and the kitchen was light. I put my eye to the door, but a couple of centimetres away, knowing they probably wouldn't be able to see. I just caught Auntie Mary saying, '...dreadful state, really, James, he's just worn out, so please don't wake him with your shouting.'

But Dad didn't take any notice of this. At the top of his lungs he said, 'Couldn't you have found anything *uglier* to dress my son in? Couldn't you have found anything *more* old-fashioned and uncomfortable? I'm surprised you didn't make him wear a bleeding *tie*.'

'James!' I saw Auntie Mary walk right up to my father and lay her hand on his shoulder. 'We will talk about this and I will listen to what you have to say. But *lower your voice*!'

I had never heard Auntie Mary use that tone

before. It was nearly frightening, I think it even frightened Dad, because he didn't say anything.

'William is just down the hall. And he is worn out, James.' Auntie Mary sighed. 'I don't know what you've been *thinking*, dragging him to the hospital every night. You should have left him with Helen.'

Now Dad started to cry again. 'No!' he said. 'He wanted to come. He wanted to be with his mum all he could.'

'You mean *you* wanted him with *you*,' Auntie Mary said and my dad started to cry again. Auntie Mary pushed him down into a chair. 'You've always been selfish, James. I suppose we all spoiled you, because you were the youngest. But I don't think you've really thought about the effect this has had on William.'

'Billy. We call him Billy.'

'I call him William. He doesn't seem to mind.'

Dad sniffed. 'What about those horrible clothes?'

'He needed something suitable for the funeral. And he was so... down... when he arrived...

I don't know, I just thought it would be good for him to know that people understood, that what he was suffering was something... I thought the clothes *formalised* it in a way. If you truly object, I'll put something else out for him tomorrow. The trousers need to go to the cleaners anyway, if the funeral is Friday.'

'He's not coming to the funeral.'

'Yes he is, James. I promised Meggie.'

'She wouldn't have wanted him to...'

But Auntie Mary got that bit of paper out of her cardigan again and unfolded it. Now I could see it was a letter of some kind with a list on one side and normal writing on the back. She turned it over to the normal writing and read, 'James will try and stop Billy coming to my funeral. Don't let him, Mary. Billy needs to see all my friends and will need to say goodbye to me. He thinks about things a lot, does my boy.'

My eyes filled up with tears again. I wondered when my mum had written that. It would have been months ago. The last few weeks, she hadn't been able to speak, let alone hold a pen.

There was a silence in the kitchen. I guess we were all crying. Finally, I heard my dad sniff again, even though I still couldn't see anything. I wiped my eyes on my furry, black sleeve.

'James,' Auntie Mary's voice was slow and kind, 'we all grieve in different ways. William's way is to sleep. He goes deep within himself to try and make some sort of sense of what has happened. We don't all throw ourselves about and sob uncontrollably and drink too much-'

'You've been talking to Helen.'

'I'm not getting at you, James. I'm just trying to say that William's way is more like mine. That must be why Meggie sent him here.'

'That's what I'm afraid of,' Dad half said. When he speaks so softly, it's really to himself, and I always pretend not to hear. But Auntie Mary didn't pretend not to hear. She said, 'What do you mean by that, James?'

And he said, 'Just look at you, Mary, look at the state of you. It's been over eleven years since William died and you drag yourself around... I sometimes don't know why you even bother for the joy you get out of it. You might as well just die yourself as have this...' my dad stood up and waved his arms around, '...half-life, this horrible *existence*.' He went up to Auntie Mary and stuck his face in hers. 'You quote my dead wife's words at me and you turn up your nose because I've been drinking a bit and you tell me, *me*, what my son is like? Like you've coped so well? Ha!'

Now he seemed to get up steam. He started pacing back and forth in the kitchen. I could see Auntie Mary's face and it was full of fear. 'You're only five years older than me, Mary, but you look like you're twenty years older. You hide from life, behind those horrible old lady clothes, those horrid glasses that hide your eyes. Look at how white you are! When's the last time you got a bit of sun? Your face looks like dough! You live on bits of stuff a mouse wouldn't eat. You do a bunch of so-called good works just to fill up your days.'

Every word seemed to hit Auntie Mary hard. It was like I was watching a murder, like my dad was stabbing Auntie Mary rather than just ticking her off.

He stopped in front of her and I could only see half her face. He said, 'When's the last time a man looked at you, Sis, huh? Really looked at you? Do you think William would have wanted that? If William saw you in the street right now, he'd walk right by you. He wouldn't even notice you. He hated dried-up old sticks like you.'

I wanted to run in and stop him, really I did. But I was frozen where I stood. I could only see half of Auntie Mary's face, so I only saw half of it collapse. It was like someone had pulled all the bones out of it. It just folded up. So did she, she bent forward and held her stomach as if my dad really *had* been stabbing her.

But my dad wasn't finished. 'So you'll forgive me if I don't want Billy to grieve *your way*. I want him to still want to *live* when this is all over.'

I could hear Auntie Mary cry.

Then I saw my dad look at his sister, at what

he'd done to her. He got a chair and kind of pushed her into it. He said, 'Oh hell, Mary, I'm sorry.' But she just kept crying. That handkerchief that she kept up her sleeve was getting some work – the tears just kept coming and coming.

My dad didn't know what to do. He got a glass out of the cupboard and filled it with water, and then he knelt right down on the kitchen floor at her feet. 'Drink this,' he said. And Auntie Mary did, as if she were my age and he was in charge.

But my Auntie Mary kept on crying, even after she'd drunk the water. It was like her eyes were leaking and she couldn't stop.

'I'm sorry.' This was Dad. And he *was* sorry. He was always sorry. And he didn't really mean anything by it, when he got like that. He'd done it to me, once, and although it had hurt, what he'd said, I think I knew straight away that he'd hurt himself more. And he had now, too.

He said, 'God, Mary, I'm sorry,' and then he got to his feet.

'Where are you going?' Auntie Mary asked him, 'you haven't even seen William yet.'

'How can I?' my dad said. 'How can I see him when I'm like this? What if I go off at him like I just did to you? What if I hurt him like I just hurt you?' My dad looked out the kitchen window, but I could tell from the way his shoulders shook that he was crying again.

'He's just lost his mother,' Auntie Mary said. 'He needs you.'

My dad turned around and I wished he hadn't. His face was crumpled up like a walnut. 'He doesn't need *me*,' he said. 'He needs *her*. He's never needed me. He doesn't even like me.' He wiped his hand over his face and rubbed it on his jeans. 'Why do you think I kept dragging him to the hospital? I didn't know what else to *do* with him, Mary. He doesn't speak to me. He's like a little ghost, just wandering around the house.'

'You have to just wait and listen to what he says when he *does* say it, James.'

But this made Dad angry again. 'You have him, then,' he said, 'if you know so much about him.'

But my Auntie Mary said, 'No, James. Meggie was very clear on that point.' And she reached for her cardigan pocket again.

'*Don't!*' my dad wailed.

He and Auntie Mary looked at each other across the kitchen. 'I'll see you at the funeral,' he said and banged out the door.

'But James,' Auntie Mary called after him, 'what about tomorrow?'

I could have told her it was no use. Dad never turns around once he starts. He was as good as gone. Next thing I heard was the Cavalier engine revving up and a spray of gravel.

Auntie Mary came back in and closed the kitchen door. Then she leaned on it. I heard her say, 'Oh, James.' And then I ran back down to the living room, jumped on the settee and closed my eyes.

I was just in time. She checked on me and then closed the door so softly I could barely hear the latch click.

*   *   *

The next thing I heard was Auntie Mary dialling the phone in the hall. She said, 'Helen, it's me, Mary.' And then she said, 'Oh, Helen, it was awful.'

Auntie Helen isn't Auntie Mary's sister. She's my mum's sister. But all the people in my family know each other. I think we're all pretty close. Auntie Mary and Dad lost their parents years ago. I never even met them. And Mum and Auntie Helen ran away from their parents when Auntie Helen was just a little older than me. I never met them, either. I don't even know if they're still alive.

So there's not all that many of us. There's Mum and our family and Auntie Helen and *her* family and Auntie Mary on her own. We always do things like Christmas all together – we can all fit around one table. Or at least we could. Now that my cousin Suzie is out of her high chair, it might get a bit cramped. But I guess there's room now that Mum...

Anyway, that's why it was sort of natural for Auntie Mary to ring Auntie Helen after what had happened.

Auntie Mary didn't say anything for a long time. She listened for quite a while until she finally said, 'That's an excellent idea. That would be wonderful. Are you sure you don't mind the drive?' Our town is about an hour and a half from Auntie Mary's town.

I don't know what Auntie Helen said back, but Auntie Mary listened for a while longer and then said, 'Bless you, dear, I'll see you then.' So I knew Auntie Helen was going to come and visit.

And that was all of it for that one.

Maybe I shouldn't have been listening. Maybe I shouldn't have been creeping about and listening in on people's phone calls and conversations. But how else was I going to find anything out? I mean, how else was I going to know my dad even came to see me? So when I heard Auntie Mary dialling again, I didn't turn on the television or go up to my room or anything like I should have done. I listened again.

Auntie Mary said, 'Oh, hello, Rachel. Sorry to bother you on your sermon-writing day.' And then she said, 'Actually, I was wondering. Is Mark still with you? Oh, until next Wednesday, is he? Is he there now? Could I possibly speak to him? Oh, thank you, Rachel.' A longish pause. And then, 'Mark, I was wondering if you have anything on tomorrow morning... Well, I'm afraid it's from eight clear until teatime, probably near six... it's just that William's father isn't well and I do some work at the hospital on that day... they do look forward to it so... I hate to disappoint them... You can? That's very good of you.' And so I found out that Mark would be babysitting me the next day.

Mark liked me, then. And Mum had liked me. And Auntie Mary seemed to think I was all right. I had friends at school. Mr Obaje, our art teacher, really liked me. And Auntie Helen had always liked me. It was just Dad, then. It was just my dad who couldn't bear to be around me.

I heard the hoover going upstairs and then it stopped. Auntie Mary opened the door. 'Oh, good, you're awake,' she said. 'I thought we could have lunch at McDonald's. And then you're to teach me how to shop properly, remember?' She was smiling as if nothing had gone wrong and she must have washed her face and put make-up on or something. But I could still see where her eyes were red behind her glasses.

I said, 'Do I have time to have a wash?'

And she said, 'Of course.'

And I said, 'OK.'

And she said, 'Super.'

We were both lying to each other, acting like we were all right. But that seemed like the right thing to do.

When I washed my face, I looked in the mirror and my eyes were even redder than hers.

7
the gremmie

The sun was out. I hadn't noticed. When we left the house, I blinked against it. And then I looked out across the garden, where some little purple flowers were just pushing up, to where the green hills and the blue hills stretched clear to a big, blue sky with white clouds moving as fast as sailboats. The whole world was back in colour. I helped Auntie Mary open the garage door and then I stood in front of the big old Mercedes while she edged left and right and finally got it out of the garage.

I don't know why she hangs on to that old

car. She should get something smaller, like a Fiesta or something, something with power steering that she can whizz in and out of the garage and tight parking spaces. Dad says it's economical because it runs on diesel. So maybe it's part of her money-saving campaign that she's doing for me.

All I know is that even when I'm in the front, I feel about a million miles away from her across the green leather seats. It's like I'm in a whole other car on my own. I remember when I was just a little smaller, the doors were so big and so high that I couldn't even see out of the window.

We were quiet, driving through town.

I didn't know what to say. I sort of thought I should let her know that I'd heard my dad, but I didn't want her to know that I'd seen him hurt her. So I didn't say anything. Neither did she.

At least I could see out of the window now. The sunlight came all lovely and bright. There were other purple flowers on the verges and daffodils, as well. Once, a pheasant flew in front of the Mercedes and Auntie Mary braked so as not to hit it. And then we were pulling into McDonald's.

'Are you hungry?' Auntie Mary asked.

I wasn't. I didn't think I would ever eat again. But I said, 'Yes, thank you,' because I couldn't think of what else to say.

We walked in and went to the counter.

'WelcometoMcDonald'smaylhelpyou?'

Auntie Mary blinked at the guy behind the counter. She said, 'Could we have a moment, please?'

The place was nearly empty. It was one of those huge McDonald's where there's a big playroom in a kind of glass bubble stuck on one side of the building. It must get really busy at the weekends, but at noon on a weekday, it was like a ghost town. There were about a zillion tables and only two people sitting at any of them.

Auntie Mary was looking at all the things they sell. She looked a little lost, so I said, 'Would you like a fish sandwich?' Because although she knew about lots of things, she was a complete gremmie at the whole McDonald's process. I mean a grommie. You know a grommet, a complete beginner.

Relieved, she said, 'Yes, William, thank you.'

I said, 'Do you want chips?'

'Yes, please.'

'Do you want a Coke or some coffee or what?'

'I think a Coke. I don't think this is really a coffee sort of place, is it?'

I said, 'Could I have one Fillet-O-Fish™ meal with Coke and one Quarterpounder with Cheese meal with Coke, please.'

And the guy took Auntie Mary's money and then said, 'I'm sorry, we'll have to make the Fillet-O-Fish™. Have a seat and we'll bring it out to you.'

I asked him to bring some ketchup with it and we took a seat near the playroom bubble, which Auntie Mary looked at with interest.

'Would you like to go in there while we wait?' she asked. 'I'll call you when it's ready.'

Of course, I'm way too old for the stuff in a

McDonald's playroom, but I said yes just to make her happy.

I went in and there was a big slide into a ball bath. I climbed up it like I was a zombie or something and slid down into the ball bath. There I was, surrounded by brightly-coloured balls in a yellow and red plastic world, with the sun shining through the glass bubble. I picked up the balls in my arms and let them fall back into the bath. Up and down, up and down, showering my black legs with colour.

And I started to feel better again. I shouted, 'Auntie Mary, come here.'

She must have nearly run to the door, 'What is it, William? Are you all right?'

I said, 'Have you ever seen one of these before?'

'No.'

I looked at her face, how tight it was still. And I said, 'Get in.'

She said, 'I can't get in there, William. It's for children.'

But I just said, 'Get in,' again. And then I said, 'It's OK. There's nobody watching.'

She sat down on the edge and pushed her feet into the balls. I waded over and bathed her legs with them, just like I'd been bathing my own. I said, 'Look,' and flopped back, nearly disappearing under them and when I came up, I smiled at her.

She said, 'Aren't they colourful?' And then, 'Isn't this clever?' And I think I would have had her all the way in if the guy hadn't stuck his head around the door to tell us our lunch was ready.

I *was* hungry.

It took a while for Auntie Mary to steel herself to eat with her hands. I pretended not to watch her do this. And then she was eating and I was eating and really *wasn't* watching her.

After a while, Auntie Mary said, 'Of course, this is mass-produced. But it's of a very high standard, isn't it?' And then she ate a little more and said, 'These French fries are lovely,' and then she ate a little more and said, 'I can see why you like it here.'

And I said, 'Let's have pudding,' and got us two chocolate shakes.

And we just sat there, making our straws go flat as we tried to suck the shakes up through them and smiling at each other like we'd lost our minds or something.

We got even sillier at the supermarket. Auntie Mary said, 'I shall push the trolley. And I shall tell you what we need. But you have to choose everything.'

'Can I put in things we don't need?'

She actually laughed. She said, 'Yes, but don't spend *all* our money. And watch the sugar content.'

So we were off.

Half an hour later we were at the checkout and the trolley was stuffed high with bacon and sausages and curries and naan bread and pizzas and organic tomatoes and really soft toilet paper and cream cakes and even some whitening toothpaste. The deli lady had cut stacks of slices of turkey and ham and I said, 'Fine,' whenever she mentioned the price. We had orange juice and semi-skimmed milk and apples and salad bags and the really good coffee my mum always used to buy. We had everything.

At first Auntie Mary had gasped at some of the things I'd put in the trolley, and she read quite a few of the labels before she let me put them in. But by the time we'd got to the bakery bit she'd started to get into the spirit of it and said, 'Yes!' when I got a fresh French stick. And by the time we got to the checkout, she'd pushed some lemon-stuffed olives and some ice cream into the trolley herself.

She had a moment of weakness when they told her the price, but I squeezed her hand hard and she seemed to get over it, though her hand shook a little as she signed the slip. When it was all packed and in the back of the big old Mercedes, Auntie Mary pushed the rear-view mirror over and looked at herself for a moment. She said, 'Do you mind if I stop off for a moment on our way home? I want to go to the optician's.' And then she looked at her watch and said, 'But we must be home for half three. Helen and David are coming to visit.'

'Are they?' I acted surprised. And I actually *was* surprised that my cousin David would be along. David always rings me on my mobile when he's coming around – he has to pay for most calls out of his pocket money, but when we're making arrangements, his dad pays, so he *always* rings, sometimes two or three times. And then I remembered my mobile was in my coat pocket and that it was still switched off. You have to switch them off when you go visiting in hospital.

I found it and switched it back on. And right away, it did its 'You've got messages' thing and I pushed the right buttons and listened to my dad saying, 'You OK, bucko? I'm just getting on with sorting things out. Auntie Helen's helping me.' And then him again, saying, 'I'll try you later, Billy.' And then him saying that four or five other times. At last, I got one where he said – and he must have been talking to Auntie Helen – 'Do you think he doesn't *want* to talk to me?' That's, like, seven phone calls in two days from my dad. And I didn't take any of them.

So it wasn't that dad didn't like *me*. It was that he thought I didn't like *him*.

Ohhhhhhhhh. It was all so messed up.

Then my phone rang and I said, 'Dad?' but it was David. David is about a year younger than I am and he drives me crazy, but he's all right, really.

He said, 'About time, doofus. I've been trying to ring you for *hours*.' And then I could hear Auntie Helen saying something to him and he said, 'Sorry, but I have.'

And I said, 'What's up?'

And he said, 'We're coming over, all the way to Auntie Mary's. We're in the car right now.'

I said, 'Good.' Because it was, because I really wanted to see another kid, even if it *was* David.

He said, 'Suzie's still in nursery, but our school's closed today.'

I didn't say anything. I really wasn't even thinking about school yet. I mean, somewhere in my mind I knew it was a school day, but I couldn't actually imagine going, so I couldn't actually imagine David going, either.

He said, 'I've got my football, but Mum wouldn't let me wear my boots.'

And I said, 'I don't have my boots with me anyway.'

And he said, 'Good.'

And then we both didn't say anything for a minute.

And then he said, 'OK. I'll see you.'

And I said, 'Yeah, OK, see you.'

And that was it.

We pulled up outside the glasses place and Auntie Mary said, 'I'll only be a minute. Are you sure this is OK?'

And I said, 'Sure, I'm OK.' And then I said, 'That was David. They're on their way.'

And she said, 'I won't be long.'

So I sat there and wondered. Should I call my dad back? But what if he didn't want to talk to me right now? What if he was drunk or something? What if he was crying again? Maybe I should just wait for him to call me. Maybe I should text him. But what would I write? I looked at my phone for a long, long time. I never figured it out.

8
pipeline

Those scratchy trousers were impossible to run in. After a while trying to play football properly in them, I just forgot about it and David and I sat down on a bench. Auntie Helen and Auntie Mary were in the kitchen. Auntie Helen was smoking again. She gave it up when my other cousin, Suzie, was born, and that was years ago, but when we left the kitchen she had a half-empty packet of Silk Cut in front of her. I wanted to throw them away. I mean, my mum hadn't smoked or anything and she died so quickly. I didn't want Auntie Helen to smoke. I didn't want my dad to drive so fast. I suppose I'd been thinking things like that all the time I'd been trying to play football with David. I was still thinking things like that sitting down.

David said, 'This bench is a bit wet.'

And I said, 'Yeah.'

Some kids came by, older girls. They were screaming and giggling really loudly. We watched them for a while. Then David said, 'My dad said your dad's really lost it.'

And I said, 'Yeah. He has.'

'My dad says he needs some serious help.'

But I wasn't having this. 'What does your dad know about it?'

David shrugged. 'I don't know. But that's what he said.'

'What else did he say?'

'Not much. Because then my mum told him that he'd be a lot worse, if it had been *her* that had died.'

Just for a moment, I wished it *was* Auntie Helen who had died. I wished it was David sitting in those horrible clothes and me all comfortable. But I didn't really mean it. I loved Auntie Helen. And I was going to find some way to tell her to stop smoking.

David said, 'What do you think they're doing?'

I looked up and saw Auntie Helen and Auntie Mary walking along the lane to town. 'I don't know,' I said.

We watched them walking. It was nice and sunny and Auntie Mary had her cardigan tied around her shoulders. She looked different with her cardigan tied around her shoulders.

'Are you really, really sad?'

I didn't know what to say. I shrugged. Finally, I said, 'Sometimes I just don't feel *anything*.' And then I looked at the blue sky and how green the playing field was and how the white stripes were so clean and crisp and I said, 'But I think it's getting better.'

And then I took the ball and even in my scratchy trousers, ran down the pitch and scored a blinder from about seven metres out. Well, I would have scored a blinder, but this seam on my school shoes caught the ball funny and it went completely off the pitch and under some bushes. David got it out.

And he said, 'Look, they're coming back now. Let's follow them – they might have got something to eat.' David was always thinking about food.

Auntie Mary was upstairs when we got back and told Auntie Helen we were hungry. Then Auntie Mary came back in and she had a really old jumper on and her head was wrapped up in a plastic bag and smelled funny.

'What have you got on your head?' David asked her. He was good for stuff like that; he came right out with what I always wanted to ask but never did.

But Auntie Helen said, 'It's a hair treatment. Girl thing.' And she set the egg timer for forty minutes.

Then I remembered the curries. Auntie Mary didn't have a microwave, but Auntie Helen read the back and found out that they work in the oven, too. I set the table and David poked all the plastic tops with a fork. Auntie Helen put them all in the oven. Then I thought that a big jug of water would be good, because the curries would probably be hot. The shelf the jug lived on was just too high for me to reach, but I didn't want to use the stool like a baby, so I just reached up as high as I could and – crash! – the next thing I knew it was in little bits all over the floor.

I stopped breathing. I'd never broken anything at Auntie Mary's house before. I'd always been really, really careful not to, even when I was tiny. Mum and Dad had always told me over and over that Auntie Mary's things were expensive. Even the jug had looked expensive. But it was broken all right – more than broken – *shattered*.

'Billy!' Auntie Helen said, 'Whatever did you think you were doing?'

I just wanted to drop through the floor.

But Auntie Mary was laughing. She came and gave me a hug. 'I'm so glad you did that,' she said. 'You were being far too good. I was getting worried that you weren't a boy at all.'

That's when I realised that I loved Auntie Mary. Loved her enough to be glad she was hugging me, even though her hair smelled bad and David was watching and she had grey teeth and those horrible glasses...

'Hey!' I said, 'Where are your glasses?'

And she laughed again and said, 'The optician had some of my kind of contacts in stock. I'm getting used to them again.'

Her eyes were so, so blue they were nearly purple. Purply blue. The same colour as the flowers on the lounge curtains and the swirls on the lounge sofa.

Then the egg timer went off and she went upstairs. Auntie Helen went, too. She said, 'Don't touch that oven. Don't break anything else. Don't do anything stupid or I'll skin you alive, both of you!'

David and I went into the lounge and David switched on the television. We flicked through the channels but there was nothing on but *Blue Peter*. I actually quite like *Blue Peter* and I'll bet David likes it, too, but we didn't want to watch it together so he switched the telly back off.

He said, 'There's nothing to do here.'

I said, 'It's all right.'

He said, 'Are you really going to have to live here?'

I didn't say anything.

He said, 'Your dad told my dad that you were better off here.'

Everything kind of stopped. I could hear the sound of the hoover, only not the hoover, upstairs. David said, 'Well, that's what he said.'

I shrugged. I said, 'I don't know.' I tried to think about how I would feel never going home again to my own room, to my own street and my school. To my art class with Mr Obaje. To my dad. And then I looked at David. I could tell he didn't want me to be so far away, either.

And I said, 'I hope not.' And then I felt bad, because I really did love Auntie Mary now, and I didn't want to leave her all alone again, in this big, ugly house, eating her horrible cornflakes with her horrible, thin milk all on her own.

And then I could hear Auntie Helen giggling, just like those girls had in the park. She and Auntie Mary were coming down the stairs. And Auntie Mary came into the lounge.

She didn't look beautiful, but she looked

really, really nice. Auntie Helen switched on the light and you could see that Auntie Mary was really quite pretty. Her hair wasn't grey any more. It was blonde, a kind of stripy, streaky blonde, not like my mum's, more like a lady-type lady. But it was nice and her eyes were nice and she had some lipstick on and that pink blouse she wore in Majorca.

I didn't know what to say. I kind of wanted to give her another hug, but the room seemed too big to cross.

David said, 'Wowie-zowie, Auntie Mary!' And he managed to cross the room all right. He walked all around her. He said, 'She's a whole new woman,' just like on the advertisement, trying to sound like the announcer. He wasn't very good, but Auntie Mary and Auntie Helen laughed. Auntie Mary ruffled up his hair.

And then the curries were ready and I never said anything at all. Sometimes I hated David.

*   *   *

That night I dream again. It seems like every time I close my eyes, I'm back on that beach in

North Devon. Even in my sleep I wonder if I will ever get off that beach.

I can feel the shingle under my dive boots. I can taste the salt on my lips.

Mum is holding my hand, but I can't hear her. We do scissor, paper, stone again and again she runs out into the surf, cutting through the breakers like a knife. My ears are roaring from the wind or from the sea, I can't tell.

And it's the whole thing, all over again. My mum sucks all the colour from the world and she's laughing while she does it. Then the colour spills out of the bottom of her board. She's standing up again, really tiny, way, way, up on a huge wave that never moves. I am so small on the shore that I think she can't see me, but she must be able to, because she waves.

Then, at last, my mum drops down in her lowest crouch and the wave starts to move. I think it's going to drown me again, crush me on to the shingle, but it doesn't. It arches over me like a huge, shiny oil slick, only in stripes of colour, huge bands of yellow, purple, orange, red, green and blue.

The wave arches over to the hills and my mum is on her board looking perfect, looking in just the right position, and she rides that huge, coloured wave like she owns it, like it was made just for her. Her board carves out lines of colour, red bleeding into purple in a little crimson wake, green slicing through blue to make turquoise. All the time, she's cutting up and back, up and back. She's making that big wave last, using it like a canvas, and her board is like a paintbrush.

And as it stretches, I can see what it is.

The wave is a rainbow. It goes from the sea way, way back into the hills beyond. My mum is riding the rainbow, cutting back and forth across the face, really pounding her rails. I can see how much fun she's having; her head is back and her mouth is open, laughing. Her stripy hair streams out behind her.

She stops and looks back at me, and although the colour keeps on flowing, her board is steady. I can see her face, can see the way she always looked at me. It's like she's asking me a question.

And then I know. I know what she's asking. She can either stay here with me and fade away even further and the whole world can stay grey, or she can go away, all strong, surfing away to make the rainbow.

Part of me wants her to stay, even if she is grey, even if the whole world has to die to do it. But she looks so happy up there that I just can't make her do it.

I think she wants me to wave goodbye. But I can't do that either.

My mum gives a little shrug, like she always does when she doesn't get her way with something. And then she drops down into a crouch and carves back into the rainbow.

She didn't really need me to decide anything.

She's gone.

'William! William, it's all right!' Auntie Mary was pushing my hair back off my face.

'She just went away! She just left me! Like it didn't even matter what I thought!'

'I know, darling, I know.'

'She rode off on the rainbow and...'

I blinked a couple of times.

'Take a deep breath.'

I did.

'Have some water.'

I did that, too.

Auntie Mary said, 'It's only natural, William, that you should dream of her. And besides, those curries probably didn't help.'

But I didn't really listen to her. Auntie Mary was wearing this amazing dress: it was long and thin and had ruffles all down one side where it was cut up high to show her legs. It was bright purple.

She turned bright red when she saw me looking at it. 'I don't know if this even fits any more,' she said. 'I started trying on things for Friday and got a bit carried away. I've been trying on half my wardrobe, trying on things I haven't worn for years.'

I rubbed my nose on my pyjama sleeve. 'Can I watch?'

Auntie Mary said, 'Well… er… I suppose I could use the en suite when I change…' And then she said, 'Of course you can.' We went down the hall and she said, 'Get into my bed, though, I don't want you to get cold.' She pulled back the duvet for me, even though the bed was heaped high with clothes. I climbed in and pushed my legs underneath them. They were heavy.

Auntie Mary stood sideways. 'What do you think?' she said. 'Do you think my stomach sticks out too much to wear this?'

It did a little. I said, 'Well…'

And she said, 'I thought so.' She held up two more long dresses. One was blue and one was red. The blue one had a pink flower on one shoulder. The red one was plain. 'Which one do you think?'

I liked the red one. It was pure colour. So I pointed and she went into her little bathroom. She came out again just as I got the pillows heaped up just right. It was really low in the neck part, the red dress was, and you could see quite a lot of Auntie Mary. She stood sideways and you noticed those bits even more. She said, 'What about my stomach in this one?'

And I said, 'I don't think anybody will even look at your stomach in that one.'

When she stopped laughing, I said, 'Where would you wear these dresses?'

And Auntie Mary sighed. She said, 'I don't know, William. But I think it's better to be prepared, eh?'

She rummaged around in the wardrobe a bit and came up with a dark purple suit. It was shiny and the jacket had a little belt. 'What do you think of this?'

'Nice,' I said and she went back into the bathroom. There were two heaps on the bed. One of them had all Auntie Mary's grey clothes at the bottom of it, but the purple dress that made her stomach stick out was on it as well. The other heap had all kinds of things on it, pink trousers, yellow jumpers. Even a bright green shirt with little blue flowers on it. I pushed my legs under the colour heap. And then I fell asleep again. And this time, I didn't dream.

9
the plan

The next thing I heard was a little electronic chirping noise and then Auntie Mary saying, 'Eeergh,' and a slapping sound. 'Got it,' she said, and then, 'Oh, William, I forgot you were in here. Early start this morning, I'm afraid.'

Before I thought I said, 'I know. Mark's coming over and you're going to the hospital.'

'How did you know that?'

I rolled over and looked at her. Her hair was all messed up and she didn't have any lipstick on any more, of course, but even so she still looked loads better than when I had first come.

But I wasn't really thinking that much about that. I was thinking about yesterday morning and all my listening into her private conversations. My face went red.

I said, 'I heard you talking. I heard Dad talking, too.'

And she said, 'Oh, William.' She kind of pulled me over so that my head was on her arm. She was all warm and smelled nice, like a big animal. She said, 'He loves you so much. He loves me, too. He's just not all that great at showing it, sometimes.'

I said, 'I know.'

She said, 'What are we going to do with him?'

But I didn't know.

Auntie Mary said, 'Look at the time! We'd better scoot or we'll be late. Go and run the bath while I see to your room, will you? I'll put out some clothes for you. And I'll take your black trousers to the cleaner's.'

So we did.

I got washed and dressed and was downstairs before Auntie Mary was. I heard that hoovery type sound again, even in the kitchen. Now I knew it was a hairdryer.

I got breakfast things out – bacon and eggs and sausages and tomatoes and bread and butter and milk and juice. I set the table and poured the juice. This time I could reach a jug down without breaking it. I still didn't use the stool. It's funny, isn't it, how some days you can do something and some days you can't? Ordinarily, I could have easily put that ball in the top left corner from that part of the pitch, but yesterday I couldn't have hit the side of a B&Q warehouse.

Then Auntie Mary came in and she looked really, really nice in a pair of yellow jeans and a yellow jumper. She had a scarf in her hair and that was yellow, too, with blue flecks. She had her contacts in and you could see her eyes. She said, 'Oh, my, look at all this food! I'd better just stick with toast, the way my tummy is looking.'

Just then, the doorbell rang and I went to let Mark in. He said, 'G'day, William.'

And I said, 'Call me Billy.'

And he said, 'Billy it is.'

I stood there for a moment and then I thought to ask, 'Have you had breakfast?'

And he said, 'As a matter of fact, I haven't. I don't usually wake up this early.'

He did look rather tired.

Then we were in the kitchen and he was blinking at Auntie Mary. She said, 'Hello, Mark, thanks for coming.'

But he didn't say anything. Then she looked at Mark and he looked at her. This seemed to take a rather long time.

Then Auntie Mary cleared her throat. She said, 'I'm just making some of this delicious coffee William treated me to yesterday. Would you prefer some tea?'

And Mark cleared *his* throat and said, 'No, coffee is fine.'

And a few moments later, she was running out of the door with a bit of toast in her hand. Mark was frying up a big breakfast, but he looked out the kitchen window and watched her get the car out of the garage. 'She's an amazing woman, your aunt,' he said.

And I said, 'I know.'

We ate loads. Mark especially. We fried up almost all the bacon we'd bought yesterday and a whole pack of sausages and a whole pack of vine-ripened tomatoes. Mark drank a lot of coffee and as much orange juice as I did, and that was a lot. But afterwards, he looked a lot better.

He belched and then said, 'So, what are we going to do today?'

And then I had my brilliant idea. It was one of those ideas that at first seem really silly and impossible. And then you think about them and you think, hey, maybe this isn't so stupid. And then you actually work up the nerve and say it to someone. And so I said, 'Let's paint Auntie Mary's lounge.'

And Mark said, 'WHAT? I thought you'd want to go for a walk or to the pictures or something.'

And I said, 'I *really* want to paint Auntie Mary's lounge.'

We went into the lounge and I told him all about the decorating programme I had seen and how the orangey paint and the orangey carpet had made the room look really nice. And then I showed him the purply-blue bits in the curtains and the sofa and chairs and then I said, 'And you know the really amazing thing about that purply-blue colour?'

But he knew! He said, 'It's the same colour as your aunt's eyes.' I mean, he'd only met her two days ago and I'd known her eleven years. Still, he had already noticed what took me my whole life to figure out.

Mark said, 'It's a pretty personal thing, you know, painting somebody's lounge. Do you think we ought to?'

And I said, 'Well, Auntie Mary told me yesterday this was *my* house really, that she was going to give it to me when she died. So I'm sure she won't mind.'

Mark turned away really fast, but I could still tell he was laughing. Ordinarily, when people laugh at me it makes me mad. But this didn't.

Finally, he said, 'I'd better talk to Rachel and Stephen about this. If we're going to do it, Stephen would come in handy.' He went out and used the phone. He talked so low I couldn't hear him, and I really didn't try to. But then he laughed really loud and I couldn't help but hear him say, 'Well, it was your idea to open the brandy in the first place, buddy, so you can stir your sticks and get over here.'

And then he was back and said, 'He's on his way. He doesn't have any meetings until this afternoon. We're lucky.'

But we started anyway. We moved all the furniture into the dining room (cream-coloured and just as horrible as the lounge) and started rolling up the carpet. When Stephen arrived, Mark explained the whole idea really quickly. But then Stephen bent down and looked at me, man to man. He said, 'Why is this so important to you, William?'

'Billy, evidently,' Mark said, but Stephen ignored him.

He was waiting for me to tell him, but I didn't really know what I was going to say. There was no right thing to say, no thank you or please thing that covered it. So I was stuck.

But Stephen just waited, so I had to say

something. My throat felt tight when I said, 'Auntie Mary is all alone. And I... I'm going to have to go home pretty soon. I mean, some people don't think I am, but sooner or later I *am* going to go home. And then... I suppose I wanted...' I stopped talking. I didn't really know what I meant or what I wanted.

But Stephen did. He said, 'You didn't want to think of her sitting in this horrid room all on her own.'

I sighed with relief. I said, 'Yes, that's it. Exactly.'

Stephen pulled out his mobile phone and pushed a few buttons. 'Gio?' he said. 'I need you and Marcus to stop work on that and come into town... you can get back to it this afternoon, it's an easy job... I know I told you that it was urgent. This is more urgent...' I could hear Gio squawking on the other end. 'I'm not trying to be difficult. But it's an emergency.' The squawking sound faded down to just talking. 'It's right in town, the big house on the hill. Yes, Mrs Montague's place. Bring a steam stripper and the ladders and brushes, rollers and trays. Now.' One more squawk. 'I mean *now* now. I mean in five minutes.'

He looked at me and Mark. 'Well, don't just stand there,' he said, 'Go and get the paint. Two large cans.'

We walked down into town to the DIY store, really fast. There were loads of little bits of paper with colours striped on. We went through the blues and got it between two purply-blues. One was slightly more purply and one was slightly more blue. I said, 'The purplier one goes better with the curtains.'

But Mark said, 'Yeah, but the bluer one goes better with her eyes.'

So we had the man mix up the bluer one – Dulux Bluebell Meadow – and ran back up the hill. I carried one of the cans the whole way myself, even though I had to change hands about fifty times. Mark didn't change hands once.

When we got back, Stephen introduced us to Gio and Marcus. They'd already stripped the horrible wallpaper off one whole wall and Stephen had taken the curtains down.

I said to Stephen, 'This is fantastic. Thanks!'

And he said, 'You know, when Rachel came here, no one much liked the idea of a lady vicar. Or the idea of sharing their vicar with Shallbourne. Or the idea of selling the vicarage. Your auntie made things a lot easier for us. I don't think Rachel would have been able to do it all without your auntie.'

That made me feel warm inside.

And Mark said, 'Rachel says your auntie is like a one-woman committee. She does all kinds of things around the parish. Like this hospital work she does – she takes all the library books from the patients and changes them. And she sits and talks to them and finds out just what they like to read. And she...'

Mark stopped talking. I looked up to see why and saw that Stephen was grinning at him, but not in a nasty way. Stephen said, 'Mark, why don't you help Gio here. Billy and I are going to visit Lucas and see what we can pick up.'

On our way out, Stephen looked up at the big brass chandelier and sighed. 'I suppose that will have to stay,' he said. 'I can live with that, but it's the carpet that really bothers me. We need to change the carpet as well.' He sighed again. 'Maybe we can find a big rug at Lucas Moto's place.'

But I had pulled my mobile out of my pocket and was dialling my dad's number. At last. Because at last I knew what I could say to my dad.

He must have seen my number because he answered, 'Billy?' sort of bewildered, as if he had forgotten I even existed.

I said, 'Look, I need a favour,' in the same businesslike tone Stephen had used with Gio. It was the same way Mark had talked to Stephen on the phone as well. It was how my dad talked to the people he worked with.

'What?' Dad asked. He already sounded better – maybe that was just because of the businesslike tone. Or maybe it was because we had something real to talk about.

'I need... hang on... how much?' Stephen held up ten fingers, twice. 'Dad? I need twenty square metres of nice carpet. It's for Auntie

Mary's lounge. I'm doing it up for her as a surprise and we need it fast.'

There was a pause. And then Dad said, 'What colour?' The way he said it, he sounded almost like he usually sounds.

And I said, 'It has to match, or at least come close to, Dulux's Bluebell Meadow.'

And Dad said, 'Leave it with me.' Really short, really sharp, like he was awake, like he had ten million things to do, but they would all get done and your thing would be one of them. That's the way my dad usually sounds, and sometimes it bugs me. But right then, it didn't bug me at all. It was great to hear him sound that way.

I said, 'I have to go out, but there's um... loads of people here to take delivery. So... you can just bring it when you find it. And er... I'll be back here pretty soon, anyway.'

And Dad said, 'I'll be there.' We both listened to each other breathe for a little while, and then he said, 'I'll get right on it.' And the phone went click.

Now, I know that doesn't sound like much of

a conversation, written down like this, but a whole lot had happened during it. It was like my dad and I had learned how to talk to each other. And the very best bit of it happened when we weren't saying anything at all. And even better than that, *I'd* done it – all of it. Dad hadn't even known how to start talking to me – not really. But I had known how to start talking to him. And that's when I knew that it was going to be all right.

My eyes filled with tears again and I had to wipe them on the sleeve of my top. I said to Stephen, 'We'll have it in time, don't worry.' And Stephen smiled like he was trying to crack his face in half.

He called to Gio, saying, 'You'd better get on that paint right away – and put the dryers in. We're laying carpet in here this afternoon.'

Gio rolled his eyes. 'Anything else I can do, boss?' he asked. 'Magic lamp? Three wishes? Does Cinderella want a new dress?'

But he was smiling, too.

10
mr moto

Lucas Moto's place was about a half-hour away and we listened to the radio all the way there. When we got there, it was a shop full of just little bits of stuff, curtains and cushions and furnishing fabric on rolls and little lamps and shades and things you put on your walls and things you put magazines in. It was all little bits of things you never think about, never think about actually going to a place and buying. There was a huge stack of baskets. I never thought about actually going to *buy* a basket. They always just seemed to be *there*.

But this is where you came to, I suppose, if they weren't.

Lucas was an elegant-looking man in a black suit. He had long, blond hair, which was obviously dyed, not just because he was Japanese, but also because he had black roots and black eyebrows. That sounds like he looked a mess, but he didn't. He looked like he was someone important, like he should be on the telly or something. He was sitting at a desk which was covered with bits of paper and fabric and carpet samples, about a half a metre deep, with things falling off onto the floor. And he was talking on both his land line and his mobile at the same time, in English and in what sounded like Italian. He waved Stephen in. He attempted to cover the mouthpieces of both his phones and said, 'You'll just have to rummage. I'm absolutely *swamped*.' Stephen only nodded.

We went up a spiral staircase to the next floor. It was a huge space, just stuffed to the rafters with, well, with *stuff*. Stephen pounced on some purple velvet cushions. They had gold buttons in the middle and little purple and gold tassels at each end. 'Look at these,' he said. 'Now, they aren't to *my* taste, but I think they'd be great in that room. They'd even help with the brass chandelier.'

I thought they were beautiful. Stephen said, 'Oh, there's only eight of them. Well, they'll have to do.' I looked at the price tag. They were £40 – each.

I said, 'Stephen, who's going to pay for this?'

But he said, 'Don't worry. I owe your auntie.' And then he said, 'Isn't there a horrible big wood unit in that room?'

I nodded.

He held up a tin of something. He said, 'We'll make that gold, too. Can you remember what the handles are like?'

The total came to £411 pounds. Lucas Moto was so delighted he nearly put one of his phones down.

I was scrubbing the unit with a wire brush – with the grain, never against it – in nice long strokes, when my dad came in. He stood there for a while.

I didn't look at him. I just kept working.

He cleared his throat and said, 'They've nearly finished rolling the walls. The skirting is almost dry. I'm going to stick around and lay it myself.'

I looked up then. He looked a lot better than he had the day before. He was showered and everything. I said, 'Brilliant,' and looked back at where I'd been wire brushing.

He put his hands in his pockets. 'What's going on with that old thing?'

I said, 'There's this goldy-coloured waxy stuff. You rub it in. It dries quick.'

Dad said, 'Do you want to see the carpet?'

I said, 'Sure,' and we went out to where he had one of the vans in the drive.

He opened up the back and peeled some paper off the carpet roll. He said, 'I was lucky. We nicked it from a hotel job. They'll only be delayed a day.' It was a little darker than the paint, almost the same colour as the velvet cushions. It felt almost like velvet, too, smooth.

I said, 'Nice one, Dad.'

And Dad said, 'Well, I shouldn't just stand around. Have you got another wire brush?'

We did, so he went to work on the other side of the unit. We didn't say anything for a long time, but I could hear him breathing, hear the strokes he was making on the other side. He wasn't breathing heavily and he didn't smell bad or anything. I reckoned Uncle Ray was wrong. Dad wasn't going to fall completely apart.

When we met in the middle, we talked about me doing the front bits until they met up while Dad did the higher-up stuff. That was all we said, but it didn't feel horrible, it felt fine. And somehow meeting my brushed bits up with Dad's brushed bits felt really good to me, like we'd done something more together than destroy the surface of an old unit; like every one of those brush strokes heading towards each other was really important.

At last we were ready for Stephen. Dad and I went into the kitchen to do the washing-up while Stephen waxed the unit and changed the handles. It was nearly lunchtime and the plates were disgusting, all the egg was really hard on them. Mark and I had forgotten all about our breakfast things.

I washed and Dad dried and put away.

At last he said, 'Billy? Can I ask you something?'

And I said, 'Yeah.'

And he said, 'Are you doing up the lounge because you want...' but he sort of trailed off.

At last I turned and looked at him, really looked at him, looked into his eyes. They were rimmed red with crying, just like mine had been yesterday, just like Auntie Mary's had been yesterday. I said, 'When I come home, Auntie Mary will be all alone again.'

And my dad's eyes filled with tears again. He said, 'Are you sure you want to come home?'

I said, 'What do you want?' And then I held my breath. My dad dried the plate he was holding really slowly and then he put it away. And now I know what it's like when you're waiting a long time for someone to say something, because it seemed forever.

Finally, he said, 'I want you to come home.'

And then I was crying and he was crying and we were hugging and crying and I don't know how we would have stopped if Gio hadn't stuck his head around the door and said, 'Yo, carpet man, we're ready when you are.'

Well, it went fast after that. It was like a video on fast forward. Mark helped Dad lay the carpet and Mark must have been pretty good help because Dad didn't shout at him even once and he *always* shouts at anyone who tries to lay carpet with him.

Stephen and I started carrying in furniture because Gio and Marcus had gone back to their other job. I don't know what had happened to the furniture, but it seemed a lot heavier than it had in the morning. I was glad when Dad and Mark were finished and could help. Stephen moved things around about a hundred times, and I thought if I had to help move the sofa one more time I was going to scream. But at last everything was in place.

Stephen looked at his watch. He said, 'Flowers. We need flowers.'

Mark said, 'I'll go,' and he was off before any of us could say anything else.

Stephen asked me, 'Where does your aunt keep her vases?', but I didn't know. We all went into the kitchen and looked high and low. Finally I found three and pulled them out. One was clear glass and looked really elegant – the glass was thick and it was big and heavy and straight with a kind of wave at the top. One was a lot lighter and was made out of pottery or something. It was greeny-coloured with purpley bits and rosy-pink bits swirled in. Then there was a cut-glass one, all knobbly in a round kind of shape.

I put them on the table and said, 'Here, look.'

And Stephen said, 'Oh, my God, look at that! Is that what I think it is?'

Dad said, 'She's got a book upstairs… let's check.'

They raced upstairs, so one of the vases must have been really important.

Mark came back with this armful of... things. I mean, some of them were flowers, but some of them were twigs of dogwood blossom and some of them were just... twigs. I reckon they didn't have many flowers. What flowers there were, were pink, either light pink or a deep rosy colour. I said, 'These are the vases.'

Mark pointed at the round, cut-glass one and said, 'Well, that one definitely won't do,' and so I grabbed it and went to put it back. But my hand must have slipped or something, because it fell on to the tile floor with a crash.

I thought it was sort of interesting that it just smashed in half, and didn't shatter like the jug had the day before.

Stephen's voice was outside the kitchen door. He said, 'What was that?'

'One of the vases,' Mark said.

Stephen's voice shook as he said, 'Wh-which one?'

'The round one,' I said. 'I'm really sorry...'

'Thank God!' Stephen said. 'Look!' He was holding a book open to a picture of the swirly, pottery one. 'It's worth thousands,' he said. 'I wonder what other hidden treasures your Aunt Mary has.'

For some reason, we all looked at Mark. And his face went red.

Mark put the flowers and twigs in the really good vase. Stephen put them on the unit, first on one side and then on the other and finally in the middle. He plumped up some cushions. He said, 'I wish we could have boxed in that television.'

The daylight was fading and Stephen turned on the chandelier, and used the new little round knob to get the light level just right, so it was nice and warm-looking, but not glaring. We all just stood there and looked around for a moment. Then we looked at each other and we all got these big, goofy grins on our faces.

Just then Auntie Mary opened the door. She said, 'What?' and, 'Oh, James!' And then she started to cry. 'It's so beautiful,' she said. 'Whose idea was it to do this?'

And Stephen and Mark and my dad all said at the same time, 'Billy's.'

11
alone on the shore

I went home with my dad that night. I never did pick up the scratchy trousers from the dry cleaner's. Instead, I just wore chinos and a nice shirt and my school blazer to the crematorium. It was packed. Dad and I sat in front with Auntie Helen and we couldn't help looking around to see all the people coming in. It was sort of horrid to keep seeing the coffin right there, but it was kind of nice, too, to know that Mum wasn't entirely missing this, that part of her was there, the part she left behind.

There was a moment when the whole place got quiet and then got even noisier again. I half stood up to see who had come in and there was an elegant, blonde woman in a sharp, purple suit that shimmered. She wore matching, high-heeled shoes. And she had my Auntie Mary's face. Mark was with her. They came right down and sat down across from us. Auntie Helen nudged me in the ribs, 'Who's that?' she whispered.

'Mark,' I whispered back.

'Thought so.' She turned and whispered in Uncle Ray's ear.

The vicar said a lot of nice things about my mum, even though he didn't really know her. Then Daddy Cool got up and talked about her life as a surfer – he used words like 'tenacious' and 'daring'. The vicar read a poem about motherhood that Auntie Helen had picked out.

It wasn't easy to listen to all of it. Sometimes I cried and Dad held my hand. Sometimes he cried and I held his. During the poem my Auntie Helen hugged me and then cried really hard, and Uncle Ray held her. When the coffin began to roll away, I was OK, really, and so was Dad. So I had time to notice that Auntie Mary had started to cry really hard and that Mark had put his arm around her.

And then the vicar said, 'Sometimes we sing a hymn together now, but James has chosen other music for us to sing. The words are on the back of the order of service.' He pushed a button and I couldn't believe it.

It was the cheesiest surf music of all – the Beach Boys – and it was really loud, filling the whole hall. There was a murmur of surprise and everybody looked for the words.

It was called *Little Surfer Girl*, and it's a sappy little song, really, but with these killer close harmonies. I always liked it. And everybody in the chapel sang it that day, even people like me who don't sing very well.

I looked at my dad and he had tears running down his face, but he was smiling as he sang, 'I have watched you on the shore, standing by the ocean's roar...' Dad had a pretty good voice and

I could hear him singing, even over the music.

It made me smile. Because the amazing thing was, he wasn't even looking at the booklet. Dad must have listened to that cheesy song over and over, plenty of times, because he knew all the words. I looked around. Everybody was smiling. Mum would have loved it.

At Auntie Helen's house all Mum's surfer friends kept coming up and telling me that they would take me out when the weather got better if my dad said I could. And he kept saying, yes, of course I could, and handing out cards with his mobile number on.

Dad and I talked to Daddy Cool a lot. Daddy Cool is this guy who's been surfing Newquay for, like, ever. He was Mum's first coach and she always bought surfing stuff through him. His shop has everything, and what it doesn't have, he can get.

We bought my boards there. People still gave my mum boards to try. She used to say one good thing about being an ex-pro is that she'd probably never have to buy another board in her life.

And she didn't.

Dad and I arranged that when we got the ashes back, Daddy Cool would paddle way out and sprinkle them into the sea. We told Dad he would have to suit up and paddle out with us when we did it. He said he would think about it.

I talked to about a million zillion people. It was a great party, tons of different foods and things to drink. Auntie Helen thanked Auntie Mary over and over for paying for the caterers until Auntie Mary told her that she didn't want to hear anything about it ever, ever again. And they laughed.

Dad stuck to the orange juice, but he was walking around with a big bottle of champagne, making sure anyone who wanted some had it.

Finally, Auntie Helen and Uncle Ray and Auntie Mary and Mark and me and my dad all went back to our house for a little while. They had about fifty cups of tea together and I sat on the floor and kept the fire going, because it got cold when the sun went down.

They talked of this and that, over my head, about the people who had been there and how they looked and what they'd said, mainly. Sometimes Mark would ask questions about people and everyone would laugh and talk all over themselves, answering. He asked about Daddy Cool and Dad said, 'He's a pretty amazing guy, actually. He was a guitarist until he injured his hand in a factory accident. He went to California with the compensation money and... well, I reckon he just about started surfing in this country.'

Which doesn't sound all that great written down, really. But you see, before, Dad had always referred to Daddy Cool as 'that fat old creep who's always ringing'. So, it was a bit of a change. I think it had made a difference when he was ringing to talk to Dad himself and not to Mum.

Then Mark said to Mary, 'We should go off to Newquay tomorrow and buy me a board to take to Ascension. From Daddy Cool.' He said 'Cool' like a Californian, 'Kewl'. He said, 'I've heard there's some great surfing on Ascension.'

Auntie Mary squeezed his knee. She said, 'We'd have to be up with the larks, it's a long drive.'

And I asked, 'Where's Ascension?'

And Mark said, 'Ascension Island. It's in the middle of nowhere. I'm off on Wednesday to hang out with the turtles.'

I looked at Auntie Mary, but she was still smiling. It was Auntie Helen who started to cry.

Auntie Helen said, 'You're *leaving*? Wednesday?' And she just buried her head in Uncle Ray's shoulder and sobbed, really big tears that ran down her face.

Mark looked at me and then at Auntie Mary. She squeezed his leg again. She said to Helen, 'It's not easy to even get a flight to Ascension Island, Helen. And it's Mark's job.'

But Auntie Helen just cried and cried. Uncle Ray looked at us all over the top of her head. He gave a little shrug. He knew she was acting strange, that she'd just *met* Mark, and that if anybody had the right to be upset about him leaving it was Auntie Mary. We all knew that.

But still, he held on to Auntie Helen and just let her cry, as if she was being reasonable.

The rest of us looked at each other. Dad looked confused, but Auntie Mary was kind of smiling. She pushed at Mark, as if he should do something.

Mark came and sat on the rug by me, right at Auntie Helen's feet. He reached out and jiggled one of her ankles and she looked up, wiping her eyes with the back of her hand, which smeared black stuff all down her cheeks. He said, 'Helen, everything changes.'

And she said, 'I know. But *why*?'

Mark shrugged. He said, 'I'm just a stupid animal guy. I can't tell you that. But I remember at uni they told us either an organism is changing or it's dead.' He coughed, like it was bad to say the word 'dead', like we hadn't all been thinking 'dead, dead, dead' all day. He shrugged again. He said, 'Change is life, Helen.'

She sniffled again. I stepped over Mark and went and got some kitchen roll for her. She said, 'Fanks,' and wiped her face and blew her nose. She looked at Mark and said, 'Yeah. Yeah, I suppose so.'

And Uncle Ray just beamed at Mark like he wanted to take him outside and give him a million pounds.

Auntie Mary said, 'Mark's going to an island in Greece after he finishes on Ascension. More turtles.'

And Mark sat back down by her and said, 'And you're going to meet me there, aren't you?' Auntie Mary smiled with her whole face, her bright blue eyes shining. Auntie Helen smiled, too. And Mark took Auntie Mary's hand and held it, like he'd just earned it.

Dad and Uncle Ray looked at each other and shook their heads. You could almost hear them say 'Women!'

I got a tight feeling in my chest that felt almost *too* warm, like I was *too* happy, with everyone around and being good to each other. Like I almost couldn't handle it. So I got up and put the kettle on again. Dad helped me wash up the dirty things.

And they all drank another fifty cups of tea.

Auntie Helen and Uncle Ray had to leave first, to go and pick up David and Suzie and make sure the house had got cleaned up properly. Finally, Auntie Mary and Mark left, too.

Auntie Mary hugged me before they left. I wanted to tell her that she looked wonderful. I wanted to ask her when I would see her again. But all I could think of to say was, 'Thank you for having me to stay with you, Auntie Mary.'

She bent down to look in my face. And then she hugged me again, really hard, and kissed me. I didn't mind.

She said, 'I love you, too, Billy...' And I didn't mind that, either.

It was hard to let her go.

My dad put his arm around my shoulder and we watched Mark reverse the big car out of our drive. Then we just stood there and watched the red tail lights until we couldn't see them any more.

I leaned my head on my dad's arm and we looked up at the stars. I knew we were both wondering if Mum was up there somewhere, looking down to see us. My eyes filled up with water and my nose wanted to run.

I sniffed a little. Dad's arm hugged me a little tighter. The night air was cold, but my heart beat warm inside my chest. Dad laid his big hand right over it, as if he wanted to feel it beating. And then we just looked at the stars some more.

We didn't say anything.

We didn't have to.